The Truth About Hazel?

Mary Thurlow

First published 2019
by Rowanvale Books Ltd
The Gate
Keppoch Street
Roath
Cardiff
CF24 3JW
www.rowanvalebooks.com

A CIP catalogue record for this book is available from the British Library.
ISBN: 978-1-912655-45-8

This book is dedicated to my mother, Amy,
who always believed I could write.

Special acknowledgements go to the following:

My husband and best friend, Michael, who said,
"This is our time. Go for it,"; my good friend, Jan,
who typed out my scribble and was always so
encouraging; and to Barbara and John, our good
friends in Norfolk, who were always so positive.

CHAPTER 1

"I remember Hazel."

"Pardon?"

"The person your story is about. Don't you remember her? She caused quite a stir in the community at one time. I think she lived quite near you."

"Of course."

Let me explain. As a novice writer I am often unsure of my abilities, and I used to invite my closest friend round for lunch and to read my latest work.

That Wednesday, we had exchanged news and gossip, shared a light meal of salad and crusty bread, a few glasses of white wine, and then I gave Sue my story to read.

"This is only the first draft of the opening chapters. Obviously, I shall rewrite some of it, flesh out some of the ideas as I go along, but cast your beady eye over it and tell me what you think. Make some suggestions if you will, but make them positive. I wilt with too much negative criticism and lose all impetus."

Sue smiled. We had known each other for some time—started college together, got married the same year, began our teaching careers in the same school, and our first children were born within days of each other. But she had stayed in teaching whereas I left after about ten years. It wasn't for me.

I had various odds and ends of jobs and then ended up back in a school, this time as a secretary. There I stayed for fifteen years until, at the age of fifty, I decided to concentrate on what I had always wanted to do, which was to write. My three children were adults and Gerry, my husband, gave me his blessing: "Go on. Go for it."

So I did, and had a few short stories published. I walked on air for a while; I could be a genuine author! Then self-doubt set in. I wanted to write a full-length novel, but after ripping up various attempts to start the thing, I rang Sue and asked her if she could come over and read through my stuff.

That Wednesday, after we had enjoyed our lunch, I cleared the table and took the dishes into the kitchen to wash up. When I returned, Sue had read a few chapters and made some comments.

"That's a fair point," I mused. "I rather left that hanging in the air, didn't I? I should go back to that and give some kind of explanation. Or perhaps write a prologue. Thanks for that."

Then Sue said, "Strange you should call your protagonist Hazel. I remember Hazel."

As she spoke, the cobwebs cleared in my brain. Gosh, I remembered Hazel, too.

"Fancy me choosing that name! My subconscious butting in," I laughed. "I suppose I'll have to change it. Especially if she's still alive."

"She could be, you know. I wonder where she went to; she sort of disappeared. But it was all a long time ago. Your character reminds me a bit of the Hazel I knew. There was something mysterious about her, some sort of scandal—I can't remember what. Then she moved away. You knew her better than I did."

A host of old memories surfaced. "Yes. She was friendly with my mother when she lived two doors away from us. I was only young. Fancy forgetting her. It's all coming back now."

"It's like snapshots," Sue said. "Someone mentions a name, or you smell something, or you hear a tune, and you suddenly remember something that was hidden deep inside your brain."

I nodded. Pictures were coming to life in my mind.

After that, Hazel's image started to come to me at odd times of the day and night. When I was washing up, ironing, cleaning the toilet—those domestic chores when I didn't need to think—my mind would drift, and I would see Hazel before me clearly.

She had a small, round head of dark brown, curly-ish hair and a face of sharp features. She reminded me of a bird. I'd often heard her singing as she pegged out her washing in the back garden.

Her husband, Lance Taylor, was a big bear of a man with a cheerful disposition. He was always rushing about, mowing old ladies' gardens, delivering things, acting as a taxi service to anyone sick or whose car had broken down. If anyone needed anything—hammer, saw, strimmer, hedge trimmer—one only had to ask Lance. If someone's car refused to go, he would be the first person under the bonnet. Everyone liked him.

I remember the day he died as if it was yesterday, the story told by Hazel to my mother and later recounted to me. Hazel had come home from shopping, put her bags in the kitchen, kicked off her shoes and turned on the television. She had missed the national news but caught the beginning of the local programme. There had been an accident on the M4. Three cars had been involved. Four people had died. At that moment, the doorbell rang. Hazel opened it to find two policemen on her doorstep, and then she fainted.

When she came to, she was lying on her sofa, one policeman kneeling at her side. As her eyes opened, he offered her a glass of water. The other officer sat in the armchair opposite. He spoke to her gently.

Hazel came to our house, two doors away. Her face was grey. My mother sat her down and shouted to me to put the kettle on.

The sad thing was that Lance had been giving a colleague a lift to work that day and had been a little later than usual joining the motorway because he'd had to pick up his colleague first. If he had left home the usual time and joined the traffic ten minutes earlier, he would have avoided the smash. His colleague was a dad with three children.

And Hazel had just discovered, that very morning, that she was pregnant.

Hazel remarried very quickly. So quickly that my auntie, and plenty of others too, considered it indecent, but my father remarked that it was probably to give the child a father. Her new husband's name was Grant Chase.

Hazel didn't wear white at her second wedding. I heard my mother whisper to a neighbour that it was because "she's not a virgin". I was pretty ignorant of the facts of life, but I knew a virgin was a woman who had not been *touched* by a man, whatever that meant. My Sunday School teacher had tried to explain this to my class once. Her face turned a deep shade of pink, and there were sniggers from some of the girls. I didn't know why they were sniggering, but I smiled, mysteriously I thought, as if I knew the joke.

Anyway, as Hazel had been married to Lance, I guessed he must have "touched" her.

The wedding dress was a deep dark shade of— well, I suppose a purplish red. It sounds ghastly, but it was rather a lovely colour. The problem was that, being pregnant, Hazel was rather bigger than the figure the dress was made for and, being made of a silky material, it did not "give" readily. So my mother was constantly altering it, letting out seams, putting in darts—I'm not a seamstress, so I don't know what my mother actually did, but it more or less fitted, albeit a little snugly, when Hazel walked down the aisle.

I had a handbag the exact colour of Hazel's dress. Well, we argued about that. In some light it was; in another light it looked paler. I offered it to Hazel for her to carry instead of a bouquet. As it was her second time before the vicar, I had thought she wouldn't want flowers. She accepted it with a smile when I took it around to her house. Perhaps she didn't want to disappoint me. But on the day, she carried a small posy of white flowers.

I was chief bridesmaid as such. I wore a patterned green sheath dress, which again sounds awful, but I liked it and felt quite glamorous. Two little girls on Grant's side looked angelically pretty in fluffy lemon creations and pale lemon boleros.

Because I'd had to be "fitted" by my mother too, I attended the same sessions as Hazel and had to wait my turn as my mother fussed around her with pins in her mouth and an anxious frown on her brow. Hazel chatted incessantly—nervous I suppose—and I found out quite a lot about her.

I learnt that her middle name was Elizabeth, a name that later brought to mind that dark purplish red dress whenever I heard it. I learnt that she had become "involved" with Grant Chase just weeks after Lance died. She had just returned to her job because people kept telling her it was better to be busy—it would take her mind "off things". I think my mother, Marion, was one of the local women who advocated this. Grant, one of Hazel's colleagues, had been only too ready to comfort the grieving widow. She had known him for some time, and his kind words melted her heart, so when he suggested going "for coffee" first, and then "let's do lunch together", she complied and was an easy touch for his "advances". Whatever "advances" were. My mother shook her head when Hazel used this word, so I could only think Grant had tried to do something awful. I worried about this for days. Wasn't an "advance" some kind of loan?

When Grant suggested marriage, Hazel was taken aback at first. But when she pondered over her future, she thought that as Grant was a nice man and all and she had "a bun in the oven"—her words not mine—it might work out quite satisfactorily. Not that she had not loved Lance, she hastened to add, but he would not have wanted her to spend years grieving over her loss.

I quite believed that. Lance was such an easy-going, hearty kind of man who lived in the moment. I guessed if he was in Heaven—wherever that was—he would be looking on with a smile when Hazel got hitched to Grant Chase.

Many neighbours did not feel that way, however, and I could quite plainly hear lots of tut-tutting from groups of gossipers when I walked with Hazel along our street. On the day of the wedding, there were little knots of grim-faced onlookers outside when Hazel sallied forth from the church on her new husband's arm.

CHAPTER TWO

I later learnt from my parents that Hazel was born a Jew and had spent a short time in a German concentration camp as a very young child. It was near the end of the war; things were pretty chaotic and some of the Nazis had fled when they heard that the allied troops were on their way. So Hazel and her mother had survived. They had both come to Britain, and—a very clever girl— she soon learnt to speak English and even went to university. There, for a while, she had been happy and quite bohemian; she had smoked and drunk and stayed up all hours, entering into debates about the meaning of life and such. Then, for no apparent reason—or none she ventured to disclose to my mother—she became disillusioned with university and dropped out.

When I heard about Hazel's past, I was intrigued. How had such a clever Jewish student ended up living in a terraced house in a South Wales village? Why had she suddenly dropped out of university in England? What had happened to the rest of her family?

My father pointed out that, by the time Hazel and her mother were captured, the Nazis knew they were heading for defeat. Even some of the guards were starving and in a pretty poor way.

He did not know what had happened to Hazel's mother. She had not told them much about that part of her life at all. My mother said that, as Hazel was only a toddler when they were rescued, perhaps she did not know or could not remember much about her mother. Perhaps she'd died. Hazel had told them that some nights she had flashbacks of standing with a lot of other people in a place with a high grey wall. Everything was grey in her nightmares. People spoke, but they did not make sense. She stood near an iron gate or something with bars and tried to understand what the people were saying, but then her dream moved on or she woke up.

My mother said that her brain was probably blotting out lots of experiences. Why, for example, she could not remember what had happened to her mother—or her father, for that matter. She could not remember the actual liberation or all the events surrounding her coming to Britain. It was all a blur. Someone had picked her up, a kind man in a uniform, she thought. She believed she was put on a boat—something that rocked about. There were so many people, so many voices talking gibberish. My mother said it was because she could not speak English that it sounded like that. And why she could not remember her early experiences. Perhaps she was too young to speak any language, so she only had visual memories in her dreams. Those fade with time.

Hazel told my parents she was fostered with

different families when she came to Britain and she attended various schools. She learnt to speak English and forgot what she knew of her native language.

My parents were very fond of Hazel. She had been through so much during her life and was still only a young woman. They forgave her eccentricities and sympathised with her when Lance died. As for getting remarried in undue haste—why deprive her of another chance of happiness?

I looked upon Hazel with a different eye after talking with my parents. No wonder they were always there for her. Perhaps no one else knew her early history. Certainly not everyone regarded her in such a kindly light when she married Grant Chase. It was too sudden, they said. It was indecent.

When Hazel and Lance had first moved to our street, Lance had driven a huge American car. It was an old-fashioned contraption, two-toned, dark blue and a paler blue. It seemed to reflect his personality—larger than life. The trouble was it was too big for our narrow street. It seemed to lord itself over our neighbours' small boxy cars and shouted at them with an awful cacophonous horn. But when it revealed its impotency in manoeuvrability, it could not hide. Like a leviathan it took up more than its allotted space outside their house, and everyone sniggered at Lance behind their curtains. When Lance sold the monstrosity and bought a much smaller car—an Austin 30—people nodded their heads smugly. But Lance was the first to admit his mistake and was such a nice guy that they soon began to sympathise when he laughed at himself and admitted, "I fell in love with that tank. You know how it is when you fall in love— reason goes out of the window. Then I came to my senses. But, boy, I really loved that tank." He shrugged his shoulders. "I guess we all make mistakes."

* * *

Here's a tale Hazel told my mother. When she arrived in the neighbourhood, she went to the local surgery to see the GP about contraception. She found the situation unnerving. There were women of different ages sitting in the waiting room. She joined them, smiling shyly as they stared at the newcomer. The glass partition opened, and the women went up one by one to give their names to the receptionist. Hazel felt all eyes were upon her as she approached the partition and spoke to a woman in a white coat. The others were probably only interested because she was a new face in their small community.

As they waited for the doctor to begin the clinic, they chatted in an uninhibited way. The noise level rose. So did the temperature. The air became stuffy with the heat from the women's bodies, and Hazel began to feel more and more uncomfortable sitting there in her woollen coat.

The heat and the noise made her giddy and sick.

When it was her turn to go in, she stumbled through the door and was glad to sit down on a chair in the cooler, white-tiled room.

The doctor asked her if she felt all right. Hazel nodded. The doctor admired her shoes, presumably to put her at ease.

"I used to wear flat shoes and sandals," Hazel said, "but then I had trouble with my foot, and I find small heels better. And of course, I'm short, so they give me a bit of height."

"I like sandals," said the lady doctor, lifting her foot to show that she was wearing ropey Roman-style sandals herself.

"Yes, I used to wear ones like that."

Shut up, Hazel, she thought. *What the hell am I doing, gushing on about shoes?*

She cleared her throat. "I'm a new patient and I've just registered with you."

She rummaged around in her large brown bag. She was sweating, and she could not find the manila envelope from her last GP. She took out her purse, her comb, some old bills and receipts, a make-up bag: all the paraphernalia that usually finds its way into a woman's handbag. She could not find the damn thing. Had she forgotten to bring it?

"Is this what you're looking for?" the doctor asked and pointed to the desk.

Hazel almost threw the Gladstone bag to the floor. Had she had the envelope in her hand when she came in? Had it been in her pocket? She did not remember taking it out. She began to put all the things back into the bag, blushing, and then sank down small on the chair, feeling silly.

The doctor crossed her legs and smiled, trying to look friendly.

Hazel took a deep breath. "I've come to see you to make arrangements about contraception."

If the doctor thought to herself, *Why, surely that's why you've come to a contraception clinic*, she said nothing. Continuing to smile, she asked Hazel what contraception methods she and her husband had used previously, made some notes, and told her to report to the receptionist, who would give her some emergency condoms. Hazel stood up, knocked the chair over, grabbed her bag and the note from the doctor, and left the surgery in a hurry, not looking to left or right. A maelstrom of emotions were passing through her and she just wanted to get out into the fresh air as quickly as possible. She certainly wasn't going to ask for condoms with all those other women watching and listening.

Later on, she learnt that the doctor was very wise and competent and a sincerely nice person and that the village women were, for the most part, friendly and kind, if a little garrulous. But Hazel didn't like people knowing all her business, and she never went back to the contraception clinic.

My mother smiled when Hazel told her the story and sympathised with her feelings. As an outsider with an English accent, Hazel rather stood out in our small community, and the local people wanted to find out all about her. They were nosy, but they meant no harm. They criticised everybody—but not to their faces. They had their opinions but did not wish to offend. It was just that everyone had to know his or her place.

Hazel would learn that in times of trouble, the villagers always came together. That was good. It was how a community should work. But she was never open with her business with anyone but my parents. They were more tolerant than most of our neighbours, and non-judgemental. As staunch chapel-goers they believed in the Christian values of forgiveness and love for one's fellow man. As ordinary, working-class folk they knew life could be hard for many people, and they liked the shy young woman who'd had such a difficult start in life.

Hazel told my mother she knew Lance wanted children, but she wasn't sure. She liked her independence and didn't want to be tied down with a child. At first, she worked in a local bakery and got to know the locals better, then she did a typing and shorthand course and went to work in an office in Cardiff. By the time she decided she would like to have a baby with Lance, it was too late. He was taken away from her.

She wept in front of my mother because she missed her best friend in all the world. She wept because he would have made a wonderful dad. She wept because her child would never know what a good man Lance was.

CHAPTER THREE

When Hazel and Lance had lived two doors down from us for a while, the big bear of a man did something stupid. He had an affair with a silly young girl who worked behind the bar at the Working Men's Club. Then he felt guilty and put a stop to the relationship, but his guilt ate away at him until one evening he confessed to Hazel on bended knee. She was bitterly upset and sobbed her heart out. Lance could not bear to see her pain. The next day he packed a suitcase and drove off in his Austin 30.

After he left, Hazel was distraught. Despite the fact that he had betrayed her, she wanted him back. She told my mother that if he returned, she would forgive him everything.

She looked for him everywhere. She caught buses and travelled from village to village, from town to town, showing his photograph to strangers in pubs, clubs, hotels, cafés and libraries. They would look at the creased snapshot and hand it back, shaking their heads. Our neighbours got to know about her search and scoffed, "She'll be putting up a wanted poster next."

She told my mother she was having nightmares.

"Can't you register him as a missing person?" suggested my father.

"I don't want to get the police involved. And he's left me. He's not really 'missing' as if I don't know where he's gone."

"Yes, but you miss him, don't you? He's missing to you."

"He's probably gone to Cardiff," said old Mrs Davies from number nineteen. "She'll never find him if he's gone there!"

My mother was wiser than old Mrs Davies. She gave Hazel a cwtch and said confidently, "He *will* come back, my love, I'm certain of it. And then the nightmares will stop."

Hazel bit her lip. "Do you think?"

"I know."

And come back he did. His car was outside Hazel's house when I came home from school one day.

Hazel told my mother a few days later, "He missed me, Marion. He was so upset at what he'd done. He told me it was only the one time, and he knew it was madness. A moment's madness. And he was so sorry he'd hurt me."

"It would have been better if he'd never told her," my mother said to my father.

"Better for them both if he had never had the dalliance in the first place," declared my father.

"What does dalliance mean, Dad?" I asked from the doorway.

"You get on with your homework and don't eavesdrop," I was told.

"What's eavesdrop?" I asked, feigning innocence.

Hazel was in my house again a few days later, having a cup of tea. I threw my satchel in the corner and said hello before dashing off to the outside lavatory. When I came back, Hazel was saying, "He made a mistake, Marion. We can all make mistakes. I'm just so glad he's back. The world was so grey without him." She gulped.

I busied myself with washing and drying my hands in the washhouse, but the door was open and I was listening to every word.

"I couldn't bear the nightmares. When we were first married, I had them, and Lance would wake me up and then it would be all right. He'd rock me like a baby. And everything would be all right."

"Have the nightmares gone now?" My mother glanced up and frowned at me. I slunk back but kept my ear to the door.

"Oh yes. They've gone."

"Thank goodness for that. Let's hope he never makes the same mistake again."

"Oh, he won't. He's promised me." Hazel lifted her big, brown, watering eyes to my mother's face. "He's promised me," she repeated.

"Well then, he won't," my mother concluded. "Have another cake."

Lance was a contrite husband. For a little while he shunned the neighbours, knowing they were gossiping behind their curtains and condemning him as a cheat, an adulterer, a love-rat and lots of other common expressions.

Gradually, life settled down, and Lance recovered his composure and his usual joie de vivre. He seemed to work twice as hard at helping people, even cutting old Mrs Davies's hedge, though she had made the most scathing remarks about him, sometimes within his earshot. Eventually, people stopped talking about him and were only too ready to accept his free and willing assistance when he offered his services.

Hazel seemed to look thinner and her nose looked more prominent and pointed. She looked even more like a bird. But I heard her singing as she was pegging out the washing one Saturday morning, so I knew she felt better.

And what of the young girl behind the bar at the Working Men's Club? She was "flighty", my mother said, known for flirting with other women's husbands. She became "in the family way" and got married.

My father harrumphed from behind his *Morning Star* when he heard the identity of her husband.

"Those two suit each other," he said. "He's as bad as she is. Always eyeing the women."

"Hush, Reg," my mother said. "Poor girl. She's been the talk of the village. Don't wish too much unhappiness on her."

"I'm only saying…"

"Yes, well. Anyway, as long as she keeps away from Lance Taylor…"

"He won't want her now. No one will want her now she's up the stick," my father commented, putting his newspaper down.

It seemed at times as if grownups talked in a sort of code. I often had trouble understanding everything my parents said. I would have to ask my best friend, Phyllis, what some words and expressions meant. She knew lots of strange secret things, did Phyllis.

* * *

Not long after Hazel married Grant, I heard about the washing machine incident and sort of got caught up in it myself. Hazel loved doing the laundry and hanging out her washing on a bright, fresh day, her clothes and sheets billowing in the wind. My mother had educated me from an early age on how best to hang out items so they caught the wind. I used to examine Hazel's washing on the line. She was an expert in my eyes.

Hazel's old washing machine broke down. Grant had the huge contraption out in the middle of the kitchen floor.

In those day kitchens were not fitted out with "units"—our kitchen was just another room, but as well as an armchair and a sofa, it contained a food cupboard, a kitchen range with large fire grate and side ovens, and a well-scrubbed table around which my family took all our meals. Some people covered their kitchen tables with Formica, but they were the more "modern" families. Lance had done this for Hazel. He had also taken out the old kitchen range not long after they had moved in and, instead, installed a new electric cooker. Then he had bought Hazel a new washing machine. A gleaming white, twin-tub washer.

Grant found Lance's toolbox in the cupboard under the stairs and had every tool you could think of laid out on the kitchen floor. But Lance he wasn't, and he was no expert at fixing broken washing machines.

The day wore on. The washing machine still sat sulking, refusing to cooperate, in the middle of the kitchen. Tools everywhere. Bits of machine taken off. A pile of dirty laundry in a basket sat on one of the kitchen chairs. The sky darkened and the clouds threatened rain. At least a shower. And Hazel's nerves gave out.

"Why can't you fix it?" she asked querulously.

"I don't know. I've never had to mend one of these things before," he snapped.

"I bet if it was the car, you'd have fixed it soon enough."

"I doubt it. I'm not that hot on mending cars, either!" His hair stood on end. He was getting hot and bothered. "Haven't you got an instruction book or something?"

She shook her head. "I've never seen one. But Lance got it up and running for me, and he knew a lot about machines and that. I expect he would have known how to fix it."

Grant threw down a spanner or some other such tool. "Oh, Lance this and Lance that. I'm sick of hearing about Lance! Oh, Lance could do anything, could Lance. Bloody Lance. Well, Lance isn't here and I am, and you're stuck with me!"

With an anguished look, Hazel burst into tears and fled—straight to my house to relay the argument to my mother.

"Reg!" my mother called from the washhouse door.

"What?" came the faint response from the outside lavatory in the backyard.

"Can you come here quick?"

"Woman, I'm..." There was an angry muttering and then the sound of the lavatory flush. My father stormed in angrily, still pulling up his braces. When he saw Hazel sitting in our kitchen, his features softened.

"Oh—hello, Hazel." And he ducked back into the washhouse to run his hands under the tap.

When he came into the kitchen, drying his Lifebuoy-scented hands on a towel, Mam said, "Reg, Hazel's washing machine's conked out and Grant can't fix it. Could you help her?"

"I don't know the first thing about washing machines."

"Well, could you pop over to Johnny Bracci's and ask him if his Len can see to it, dear? He's really good with mechanical things."

I caught the word "dear" and knew it was a codeword. My parents never used endearments to each other like "dear" or "darling" normally. This was an extra polite way of talking in front of strangers and would require an equally extra polite response.

My father threw down the hand towel in a gesture of resignation.

"I'll slip across now, dear, and see if he's in."

He caught me on my way through the middle room and explained the situation. "Your legs are younger than mine. Run over to Johnny Bracci's and ask for Len."

Len dutifully came. But fixing washing machines was not like mending cars, which was his forte, and the great hulk sulked in Hazel's kitchen for nearly a week, with her having to skirt around it for cooking and cleaning. My mother offered to wash Hazel's things along with ours in our old mangle-type washer, but proud little Hazel declined the offer.

Another wash-basket piled up with dirty laundry. And then a van turned up outside Hazel's door one day, and a brand-new, gleaming white, automatic, front-loading washing machine was ceremoniously wheeled in. The sulker was manhandled onto the trolley, dumped in the back of the van and driven away.

All the women in our street were envious of the new automatic washing machine. I heard whispers of, "How can he afford one of those? He must be making a bomb!" "Oh, it's probably on the never-never." "My cousin's got one. It leaked all over the floor." But Hazel was very happy with her new washer. And in time, other women had them. On the never-never, of course. Hazel and Grant got over their first quarrel, although Grant never recovered from the feeling that he was not as good a husband as Lance. He would always be second best.

CHAPTER FOUR

There were many rows after that. I often came home from school to find Hazel in my house. Sometimes I could see she had been crying. My mother would find errands for me—"Slip down the shops and get me half a pound of tomatoes/a loaf of bread/a quarter of ham…"—or she would send me straight upstairs to change out of my school uniform.

Some people blamed Hazel: "She should never have married that man so soon after Lance died." "She couldn't have known him that well." "She only married him to have a dad for the kid." "And it's not his kid, even."

Some neighbours blamed Grant: "He's not the man Lance was." "He's got an awful temper, that man. I've heard him shouting at her." "I hear he knocks her about." "She'd be better off without him."

My mother did not condemn either party. Hazel had been through a hard time, and Grant could never be Lance. They needed time to settle down. A baby was on the way. Help and support was what they needed. Gossiping would not help the situation.

"They should keep their traps shut about other people's business!" my dad declared.

"Siâni love, would you slip down the shops for me? I need some bananas."

I harrumphed and threw down my satchel, ready to go back out.

Their last row was at the railway station. Hazel walked onto the platform carrying a bag of potatoes. Customers at the local greengrocer's said she had been in some kind of trance when she asked for four pounds of King Edwards. The bag was heavy, so Hazel put it on the bench and sat down beside it. The booking office was closed and so she had no ticket. In those days you could get on the train and pay when you got off the other end. Our station was only manned part-time, so it was quite common for people to board the train without a ticket and pay in Cardiff. If you got off at one of the smaller stations or halts en route, you could travel free if their part-time staff had finished for the day. The train service must have lost revenue this way, so later on they introduced conductors who dished out tickets during the journey.

There were only a few other travellers on the platform. Hazel could see the train approaching, a long way down the track. She had decided to travel to Cardiff. Why did she have a bag of potatoes? She would leave it on the bench.

I see her now in my mind's eye as her fellow would-be travellers described her, in her shabby brown woollen coat, left open to reveal the paisley pinafore beneath. Mrs Jenkins, number ten, High Street, wondered why Hazel was still wearing her pinny.

Hazel's hair had grown long and had lost

much of its curliness. (I didn't know about perms then; my mother never had her hair curled.) It was pinned behind her ears in the fashion of the day.

Suddenly, Grant came rushing down the hill and through the gate. His belted mac flew open as he ran. The people on the platform heard him call her name. He remonstrated with Hazel, who shook her head and moved away from him, closer to the platform's edge. The other people could hear that they were quarrelling but only caught occasional words and could make no sense of what they were quarrelling about.

And then, as one witness recalled, Hazel put up her hand, possibly to ward him off, and Grant caught hold of it and bit it. She screamed—everyone heard that—and withdrew her hand. She slapped his face hard. He caught hold of her arms. The train charged towards the station. Hazel tried to run away from Grant further up the platform. Grant caught her. There was a struggle. Then Grant was not there.

The train had begun to slow, but the poor driver could not brake quickly enough. There was a squeal of brakes. Then sudden silence.

People sprang into action. There was shouting from the people on the platform. "Ring for an ambulance." "Dial nine-nine-nine." "Pull the train back." But the driver in his cab could not move. He was petrified with shock. Hazel had sat back on the bench, her face white. Passengers opened the train doors. Some alighted and stood on the platform, wanting to know what had happened.

"A man jumped in front of the train."

"No. That lady over there pushed him—I saw her do it."

"Poor bugger!"

Still Hazel sat in shock, her right hand in her mouth, the other clutching the bag of potatoes.

When the police came to take her away, one of the constables noticed her hand was bleeding.

"What happened here?"

"He bit me. He bit me," was all she said as she was led through the gate and put into the police car.

Because there were witnesses and one was adamant that Hazel had deliberately pushed Grant into the path of the oncoming train, the case came to trial. My mother was called as witness for the defence.

Hazel had been to my house earlier in the day and broken down in tears. I was in school. My father was in work; he was a checker at the colliery. No one could back my mother up, but she was known to be an honest woman and she had sworn an oath on the Bible. No one doubted her words.

"In what state of mind was Mrs Chase when she came to your house?" my mother was asked.

"She was very upset. She was in tears."

"Could you tell the court the reason for this?"

"She and Grant had had a row."

"Do you know what the row was about?"

"She could not remember how it started exactly, but it ended up with him saying he did not want the baby. She told me he said cruel things, hurtful things."

"Such as…"

"It wasn't his anyway and it would be a permanent reminder of Lance. Perfect bloody Lance—I beg your pardon, your honour—and how he wished the baby would die."

"And then?"

"She told me he started hitting her. She was not worried about herself, but she was scared in case it hurt the baby."

"Did you see any marks on her? Any bruises?"

"No, but then some men are clever. They make sure they don't mark the face, don't they?"

"Mrs Watkins, just answer the question," the judge interrupted.

The jury was shown pictures of bruising on Hazel's arms and chest plus a doctor's report to say there were also signs of faded bruises that were made some time earlier.

"Perhaps the bruising on her arms and chest could have been made during their fight on the station?"

"I don't think so. She kept pulling the sleeve of her jumper down. And she winced when she sat down as if she was sore somewhere on the body."

"You're not just making this up in light of what happened later?"

"Certainly not!"

My mother was asked what state of mind Hazel was in when she left our house.

"She was confused."

"In what way?"

"She said she was going to leave Grant. She could not bear to live with him any longer. At one point she asked if she could stay with me, but I said I would have to clear out the spare bedroom. Since my son moved out, it was used as a dumping ground and it was a mess. I apologised. She said she would go to Cardiff and that she would leave Grant a letter, but then…"

"Yes?"

"Then she started rambling about she had nothing for dinner. Grant would be angry if she did not have his dinner ready for him when he came home. She said, 'I must get potatoes,' and then she rushed out."

I had never seen my mother cry before, but when she came home from court, she broke down. She sat at the kitchen table, the scene of so many of Hazel's tears, and wept. My father had never seen her cry before, either, and he stood helpless at her side. Then, very gently and awkwardly, he put his hand on her shoulder and squeezed it.

Later that evening my mother related the scene in the courtroom.

"How is Hazel bearing up?" my father asked.

"Poor woman. She looks tinier than ever. And white as a sheet. I think she's still in shock."

"It's not every day you throw someone under a train," I said.

"That's enough!" my father said gruffly. "Go and tidy your bedroom."

"I tidied it yesterday!"

"That's enough!" my mother snapped. "Let's not add cheek to all your misbehaviour this week."

"What misbehaviour?"

My father glared. I knew I had overstepped the mark and retired quickly to my bedroom.

* * *

Hazel had been charged under her given name of Hannah Elizabeth Hezekiah, and the courtroom had heard about her early life in the concentration camp, how her mother had gone missing, and how she had been fostered out to various families.

"Why did they have to rake all that back up?" my mother complained angrily. "She didn't want everybody to know all her business. And it could bring back her nightmares."

"If some juror believes she did push Grant in front of the train on purpose, it could help in her defence, love, as a mitigating factor," my father replied. He had seen that some of the jurors had looked upset when hearing about Hazel's past.

The loss of Lance, her first husband, was also used in her defence. Questioning her about her relationship with Grant, the Prosecution Counsel asked her why she had married Grant so soon after losing Lance.

She replied simply, "Because he loved me."

"She stood there in the dock," my mother said. "This tiny woman, heavily pregnant, and my heart went out to her."

"What about her poor husband left mangled on the track?" I asked.

"He was a brute and a bully."

"Yes, but he didn't deserve to die."

"No, but…" My mother looked at me, tired of arguing. "Everybody dies, Siâni, everybody dies. It was an accident. Accidents happen every day. Every day, people die or get killed. Hazel didn't want Grant to die. It was an accident."

But not everybody on the jury believed so, and they declared Hazel guilty of manslaughter. The judge who had shown her compassion registered surprise. He gave her the minimum sentence of three years. She had caused the death of Mr Chase, but there had been no intention on her part to cause him any injury, grievous or otherwise.

My mother said there was not an onlooker in the courtroom who did not sympathise with Hazel. My father wondered if the case should ever have gone to court in the first place.

"A waste of public money. A travesty of justice. It was an accident, pure and simple. They were arguing near the edge of the platform. He bit her hand—God knows why—there was a struggle, and he fell in front of the train. Bare facts. She didn't *kill* him."

An appeal was launched almost immediately. While this was pending, Hazel was removed from prison and taken to hospital, where she gave birth to a baby girl. In view of my mother's friendship, Hazel named the child after her, only changing the spelling of the name to Marianne.

My mother was glad the baby was a girl. "She wouldn't be wanting to look at Lance's face every day. She'll never forget Lance, but at least the baby won't be a replica of him."

The Court of Appeal was asked whether enough attention had been given to the fact that Mr Chase had been the agitator in the struggle and that a doctor who had examined Mrs Chase's hand shortly after her arrest found it to be badly bitten. Puncture marks from human teeth—Mr Chase's—had broken the skin and drawn blood. The wound had required stitches, and Mrs Chase was given pain relief and an anti-tetanus injection.

The Court of Appeal was asked to re-examine a psychiatric report on Hazel, which stated that when she had been seen shortly after the tragedy, she was suffering from severe trauma. Witness statements had described her mental state previous to the incident as being "confused", "seemed to be in a trance", "I wondered why she was carrying a bag of potatoes, I think they were. She didn't seem to know what she was doing." "She still had her pinny on. She looked a mess." Statements seemed to indicate that, far from being in an aggressive state of mind, she would have been in a passive mood.

The court dismissed these arguments, but they did rule that too much emphasis had been placed on the testimony of one witness who swore he had seen Hazel deliberately push

Grant off the platform. Though three people had been convinced of this when they made their statements, on cross-examination in the witness box, two of them agreed that they had been too far away to see what had actually happened. During a struggle of the sort that had ensued at the station, a witness would have had to have been quite close to the couple and watching their struggle at the exact time that Mr Chase fell. The court declared that as the one witness was a fair distance from the action and talking to his friends at the time, his testimony was unreliable.

The conviction of manslaughter was quashed, and Hazel was freed from custody immediately. A female support officer drove her home, but she did not want to leave the house and asked only to see my mother. With the help of my parents, social services and the district nurse, she sold the house she lived in, one of the very few in our street that was not rented accommodation, and she moved away to a different area. One where people would perhaps not recognise her, even though her photograph had appeared in local and national newspapers. She had her hair cut to change the way she looked, and she changed her name back to Hazel Taylor.

"She can move on now," my father said. "She wouldn't want the neighbours gossiping behind her back and calling her a murderer or a gaol-bird."

CHAPTER FIVE

We hadn't known Hazel very long—eighteen months, perhaps two years at the most. My mother wrote to her while she was in prison and went to see her after her release, but when Hazel moved away, she left no forwarding address. My mother understood but was sad—she had become very fond of her and was concerned how Hazel would get on with looking after a young baby on her own when she had not fully recovered mentally from all the strain the past year had put upon her.

"She will need a lot of support," she told my father.

"Oh, there's social services, psychiatric nurses, district nurses, clinics—these days, young mums get more support than our parents ever did."

"But after all she's been through… She's on her own most of the time, Reg, and it's hard work bringing up a baby on your own."

My mother, always a helpful soul, moved on to looking after our more elderly neighbours, doing their shopping and little odd jobs for them, calling in regularly to see that they were all right. My father went to work as usual and joined a male voice choir. Both he and my mother were stalwart members of the Methodist Chapel in the village.

I grew up with long, skinny legs, ditched my

pigtails and had a fetching bob as I became interested in the young men in my neighbourhood. I left school, went away to college and came back home to Wales to begin my teaching career. I married a local lad who worked as a gas fitter. We bought a semi-detached house, had three children, and I was blissfully happy.

My parents, Marion and Reg, grew older and greyer. First Reg died, and then shortly afterwards, my mother died of a broken heart. I forgot about Hazel and all her woes.

Now that my friend Sue had jogged my memory, I began to wonder what had happened to Hazel when she left my street. Sue came over to join me for lunch again, read my scribblings, and then we discussed what I knew about Hazel.

"It's all come flooding back to me now. She must have always been there in my subconscious, but when I used the name Hazel for my heroine, I still didn't realise why the name had jumped out at me. I can't understand how it didn't register. Now I'm having all these flashbacks about this dark-haired, bird-like woman sitting at my mother's table."

"Why don't you write about *her*? It's an interesting story."

"No. I couldn't. She's probably still alive."

"How old do you think she is?"

"Not sure. I've been trying to work it out. She was born just before the end of the Second World War. If she was only a toddler when she was in one of those camps, that would make her in her seventies now. How did you know her?"

"She came to live near me. She had a small child. There was something mysterious about her—my mother said it was something to do with having two husbands and she had lost both in tragic accidents. I don't think she lived there very long. She moved away."

I told her what I knew.

"Poor woman. No wonder she didn't stay long in one place."

Sue lived in a small town six miles away from mine. She suggested that I ask around and she would do the same. Perhaps between us, we could find out what had happened to Hazel and whether she was still alive.

After Sue left, I reached for the telephone. A local councillor in Sue's area gave me a list of names to try. Some of them were getting on in years but might have known a young woman like Hazel in the late sixties.

First on my list was a Mr Thomas, who had been a district councillor and a "pillar of the community" in his younger days. I was told he had been considered a firebrand, espousing various causes and leading strong campaigns in his ward. Such a colourful character, he had been voted into office time and time again, even by people who voted the other way at general elections.

I told him I was making enquiries about a person who had once lived in his neck of the woods. He wanted to know if I was a journalist.

"Good God, no," I cried. "This is a personal

matter. She was a friend of my mother. I thought she might have died. Someone told me that if she was still alive you would know, and I just wanted to catch up with her."

"That's all right, then," he said. "Only I could not give any, you know, details to a journalist. I don't trust them, you see. What was this person's name?"

"Hazel. Hazel Taylor. She was a friend of my mother, but after she moved away, we lost touch with her."

"Ah, Hazel." He was quiet for a while.

"Hello, Mr Thomas?"

"Yes, I'm still here."

We made a date. I was surprised to find that Mr Thomas still lived in a terraced house like the one I had grown up in. He was still living among those who had been his constituents, and even though he was now getting on, he liked to know what was happening all around him. With all one hears about politicians, local and otherwise, having their hands in the till and all that, he didn't seem to have made a packet of money or surely he would be living in a nice detached bungalow in half an acre. Perhaps he was a genuine politician—I didn't know they existed! It gave me hope for what he would tell me about Hazel.

I was ushered in by a round old lady, slightly stooped with grey hair. Through a dark, narrow hallway we passed into a rather stuffy, what we had once called a "middle-room". It was cluttered and old-fashioned, much of the space taken up with heavy furniture. Mr Thomas sat in an armchair in front of a gas fire. He had a fine head of abundant white hair and rosy cheeks, the blush coming no doubt from sitting in front of the fire on such a warm day. I instinctively unzipped my jacket.

Mrs Thomas, I presumed it was she, indicated I should sit in an identical armchair, the arms grubby with use.

At the same time, Mr Thomas said, "Sit down, sit down, Mrs Lewis."

"Tea, Mrs Lewis?" the old lady asked.

"Yes please. Milk. Two sugars."

She bustled away.

Mr Thomas beamed at me. I smiled back. Then he became serious and looked at the fire. I presumed the interview proper had begun. I wished I had brought a pad and pencil. Or a tape recorder. But maybe that would have looked too much like a reporter and he'd have clammed up. I decided to listen carefully in case I forgot anything.

"Sorry I didn't get up. Gout, you see. Extremely painful."

I looked at his slippered feet. "Oh dear, yes. I've heard it is."

We relapsed into silence.

"I remember Hazel," he said.

I waited patiently. I thought he had fallen asleep. Then he seemed to come to.

"A troubled woman."

I waited.

"The first time I became involved with her...

Yes, now. The lady in the corner shop came to call on me. Yes, that was it. She's Indian, you know, but I have nothing against foreigners, you understand. Some of them work extremely hard. This lady, what was her name now? Patel. Yes, Patel it is. Her son runs the shop now. A pleasant man, born over here. Married a local girl. Where was I? Oh yes. She'd had some trouble with Hazel." He paused. "Yes, Hazel arrived in her shop, quite late it was. She asked for a tin of tomatoes and a box of matches. Mrs Patel showed her where to find the tomatoes and turned away to get out the matches from behind her. When she turned around, Hazel had gone. Well, she thought perhaps Hazel had been sleepwalking and maybe she should tell someone. But she didn't.

"The next time it happened, Hazel came in even later in the evening than the first time. She had a nightdress on, quite a diaphanous garment, I believe, and she had curlers in her hair covered by a chiffon scarf."

"Wow!" I said.

Mr Thomas looked at me sharply.

"I didn't know she curled her hair. I thought it was naturally curly."

"Shall I continue?"

"Oh yes."

"She seemed to be confused and again asked for a tin of tomatoes. Mrs Patel called her husband. She gave Hazel one of her cardigans to cover her up, but her husband didn't want to walk her home as she was, dressed in such a see-through nightdress. So, they also dressed her in one of his old coats that reached down past her knees. All the while Hazel said not a word. She was just passive as they put the clothes on her. Then Mr Patel took her home, which was only just up the road."

Mrs Thomas came bustling in with a tray of three cups and saucers and three plates of sliced Madeira cake. We were each handed a cup and saucer and a plate. I put the plate down on a small table alongside me and held my cup on my lap.

Mr Thomas took up his story. "Hazel's nocturnal wanderings continued, and each time Mr Patel walked her back home to her house. One night, matters turned worse. Mr Patel was in the shop on his own and had a call of nature. He slipped through into the back and called his wife. He was only gone for a few minutes. When he returned, his wife showed him the trail of destruction that had occurred between his leaving the shop and her responding to his call. A matter of minutes. There were things all over the floor. He called the police.

"A few days later, Hazel walked into the shop with a pile of tinned tomatoes clutched to her bosom. She was wild-eyed with fear.

"Mrs Patel," she said, "I found these in my cupboard. I don't know how they got there. I don't even like tomatoes. Something very strange is going on."

"Mrs Patel took the tins one by one and set

them on the counter. She led Hazel to a chair at the side and called her husband.

"Later that day, they told the police that they had found the culprit who trashed their shop. It was a young lad and they did not want to prosecute as he was so young. They knew his mother and had had a word about the incident with her. So the police took it no further.

"The Patels were very kind people. They talked to Hazel and asked her if anything was troubling her. She broke down and told them that she had lost two husbands who had both died tragically. She was so young to have lost two husbands, said Mrs Patel, and they sympathised with her, trying to comfort her. As far as they were concerned, the wanderings ceased and they had no more strange incidents."

"So, how did you become involved?"

"Well, Constable Jenkins had heard from someone about Hazel's evening journeys. One night he caught her himself. She was down by the brook, just standing still, looking into the water. When he coughed, she jumped a mile. She had two tins of tomatoes in her arms and seemed perplexed as to why she was carrying them. PC Jenkins was a bit concerned. It was a cold night, and Hazel had no coat or jacket on. He and I used to play bowls together, and he told me the tale one day and asked me if I knew the woman.

"I did, in my capacity as a councillor. Hazel had come to ask me for advice a few times and I knew her as a gentle soul. She sang in the ladies' chapel choir and most people liked her and her daughter."

"Most people?"

"Well." He paused dramatically. "There were those who said she had been involved in some scandal. They didn't know what. Most people ignored them—it was just gossip."

I waited. I put my cup and saucer down and picked up my plate.

"Of course, I found out Hazel's history. I went to the library one day to look up something for one of my constituents. I had to look through microfiche copies of newspapers, and I found the report of her trial. You did…" He paused. "You did know about the trial?"

"Yes." I nodded. "She was very friendly with my parents. I had just started in Grammar School when she and Lance, her first husband, came to our street. I was the flower girl at her second marriage to Grant Chase, and my mother went to the trial. She was a defence witness."

Snippets of all sorts of things were coming back to me. Strange how deeply buried some memories are.

Mr Thomas had no more to say about Hazel. Her night-time wanderings ceased, and as far as he knew, she was a model citizen ever afterwards and never came to his attention again. He saw her around from time to time, always with her young daughter—a bright, clever child, he heard, but she left the area a long time ago.

I thanked him for seeing me, and Mrs Thomas

for the tea and cake, and left the stuffy little room, glad to get out into the fresh air. I was sweating and took my jacket off for a while, carrying it on my arm while I cooled down.

CHAPTER SIX

PC Jenkins had died, I was told. The next name on my list, Mr Jones, the Methodist minister, had moved to Somerset some ten or twelve years ago and was more than likely retired now. The incumbent minister did not have contact details. John Patel had been too young to know Hazel. His father had died, and his mother was frail and had Alzheimer's. I didn't want to bother her.

Sue suggested we contact the care homes and nursing homes in the county. There were a few old folks' homes in the area, so I made some telephone enquiries and struck lucky with the third phone call.

"I'm looking for an old friend of my mother," I said. "I think she may still be alive. I wonder if you can help me. Her full name was Hannah Elizabeth Hezekiah. She could be under the surname Taylor or Chase; she might be calling herself Hazel."

"Oh Hazel, yes. We have a Hazel, a Mrs Hazel Taylor."

So she had dropped the name Chase. I suppose it was understandable. She would not want people to remember the name from the trial. I made arrangements to call and see Mrs Taylor at Green Acres Old Folks' Home in a Cardiff suburb.

"Her eyesight is quite poor," I was told, "and she gets confused these days, poor dear."

"I see."

"Do you think she will remember you?"

"I don't know." Would she *want* to remember me?

* * *

The residential home was a newly built, modern type, light and airy inside. Just the slightest tinge of urine that the carers had tried to disguise with disinfectant. There were deep red carpets and comfortable armchairs placed in the foyer.

I rang the outside bell, gave my name into the grille on the door and was let in. A resident shuffled past with a Zimmer frame. She wore pink fluffy slippers, had thin grey curly hair and a very lined face. For a moment, I thought it was Hazel. I smiled at her. She stopped, smiled, and then carried on.

"Hello, Maisie," a bright and breezy voice addressed her. "On your way to bingo?"

"Yes, yes. Yes, yes," the old lady replied.

The carer who had spoken to the old lady turned her attention to me. She had an open, friendly face and was a trifle overweight, her navy-blue uniform straining at the buttons. She knew who I was because it was she who had buzzed me in. She took me into a room full of old people with various shades of white and greying hair, mostly old ladies, many of whom were dozing in their armchairs. The television was on way too loud.

The carer bent down towards one old lady and said into her ear, "Hazel, you've got a visitor."

"Who is it? Is it Lance?" The voice was quivery.

"No. It's not Lance." She turned to me. "She always asks for Lance."

"Rachel called yesterday. Has she come again?"

"No, it's not Rachel." Out of the side of her mouth, the carer said to me, "She knows Rachel and she's remembered she came yesterday." Speaking normally, she asked me, "What did you say your name was, dear?"

"Ask her if she remembers Siâni. Siâni Watkins that was."

Hazel turned her face to me and suddenly I could see it was her.

"Hazel." I crouched down beside her. "Do you remember me?"

She still had the small round face with the pointed nose. Though her hair was white, it still had a wave in it. Her eyes were watery. She regarded me.

"I knew a Marion. Was she your mother?" She shifted in her chair. "Fetch me my stick, Lesley. I want to go to my room."

I stood up.

The carer helped Hazel to her feet. She turned to me apologetically. "She's not very responsive today. Perhaps she's been watching television too much and it's addled her mind. Sometimes she's quite bright. Why don't you call tomorrow?"

So I did. And the next day. I became a regular visitor, used to signing my name in the visitors' book and looking for Hazel. Usually she was either in the day room staring at the television or slumped asleep in an armchair; or, not finding her there, I would look for a carer to take me to her room, number ten. The carer, usually Lesley, sometimes a tall black man called David, would knock on her door and go in, then let me know if it was convenient to enter.

And so I entered, not only into Hazel's private room but also into her private thoughts. When she was lucid she talked about my parents or her daughter, Rachel. Sometimes she was very confused and rambled.

"I had a dream the other night."

"Oh, yes?"

I settled in a high-backed armchair near Hazel. She sat in a matching chair near the window. It was quite a good-sized room so far as these go in establishments of this kind. There was a single bed with a brightly-coloured duvet cover and a homemade lavender and cream crocheted throw on top. The bed was next to the wall facing the window so that Hazel could look outside. On top of the dresser were photographs of a dark-haired young woman I presumed to be her daughter. A side table with a tray and teacups, a chest of drawers and a round orange pouffe made up the rest of the furniture. A duck-egg and cream patterned rug lay over a brown carpet.

"You had a dream," I prompted Hazel.

"Yes. I was at a wedding party. I didn't really belong there. I knew all the people, but they didn't seem to know me. I helped to blow up these orange balloons, which were arranged in a display over the door. The people didn't know me, but they didn't mind I was there. The men were all very smart in black suits and white shirts. I remembered one. He was very handsome. He was an old boyfriend of mine; he had a lovely smile. But he didn't seem to know who I was. He only had eyes for the pretty women there. I was very jealous, and I wanted him to look at me the way he used to do. The women were all dressed in white frilly dresses. I think it was a wedding."

"It sounds like... Do you remember *your* wedding, Hazel?"

She refused to answer. After a while she returned to her dream.

"We were all sitting in rows of desks, brown wooden desks, all scratched, like in school. I don't know why we were sitting in desks. It was a wedding. And my old boyfriend was laughing with everyone. I was so happy. Then when everyone left the room, he stayed behind and came close to me. I thought he was going to kiss me. He was so handsome and manly. I loved him so much. Then he asked me who I was, and I was so disappointed he didn't know me. He was very kind, but he didn't know me. And I loved him so much." Hazel began to cry.

I reached over to hug her. She asked me for a handkerchief, and I passed her a paper tissue from a box on the chest of drawers. She dabbed at her eyes and some spittle from her mouth.

"I tried to remind him who I was, but he could not remember me."

"Was it Lance? Was the man Lance?"

She stared through the window. I thought I had lost her. She seemed to be in a trance.

"No, it wasn't Lance," she said at last. "At least I don't think so. No, it wasn't Lance. I can't remember his name. I can't remember his name."

She became agitated. I rang the pull cord to summon a carer.

Hazel struggled to her feet. "Have you seen Lance?"

Between us, David and I calmed her down, and then David put her to bed. I stood outside the room. David joined me, closing the door gently.

"What started her off?"

"She had a dream about a former boyfriend. I asked if it was Lance."

David set his mouth tight. "Try not to mention Lance. It upsets her."

I nodded dumbly and then I took my leave.

***

I handed Hazel one of the photographs that stood on top of the chest. It showed a bright-eyed, dark-haired young woman in her graduation gown with a mortar board on her head.

"Is this your daughter, Hazel?"

"Yes." She held it in her gnarled old hand and

studied it. "This was taken a long time ago. She has children of her own now." She brightened. "I have two grandchildren. A boy and a girl."

"Marianne, isn't it?"

"Marianne? Marianne who?"

"Your daughter."

"I haven't got a daughter Marianne. My daughter's name is Rachel."

"Oh. I see." But I didn't see. Had she changed her daughter's name? Why?

I spoke to Lesley, the carer. "I thought Hazel had a daughter, Marianne?"

"The only daughter I know of is Rachel. She comes regularly to see her mother. Funnily enough, you've always come on a different day."

"But I was sure her daughter was named Marianne. It was after my mother Marion."

"I don't know about that." Lesley shook her head. "Perhaps she changed the girl's name. People do change their minds sometimes."

We walked along the corridor together.

"Alzheimer's is a dreadful disease," Lesley said sadly.

"I didn't know… She seems to be so lucid at times."

"She has good days and bad days. Sometimes she tells me things—I don't know whether to believe her or not. She says she was in a concentration camp. Then she says she murdered someone—her husband. But her husband died in a car accident, didn't he? Poor Lance."

I said nothing.

"But there, her mind wanders. What it is to grow old, eh?"

* * *

I met Rachel a short while later. She was coming out of her mother's room as I was strolling along the corridor. She called out a goodbye as she closed the door. I stood waiting. I recognised her from the photographs on Hazel's dresser—she looked older, but it was unmistakably her.

"Are you Rachel?" I asked.

"Yes, I am. Were you on your way to see my mother?"

"If she's up to it," I replied. "If you've been with her for a while, I wouldn't want to tire her."

"No, she's fine. Bright as a button today."

"Oh, good." I felt awkward. "Would your name have been Marianne?"

The woman frowned. "Marianne? No. Why?"

"Oh, it's just that…" I took a deep breath and plucked up courage. "I knew Hazel a long time ago. She was friendly with my parents. She had a daughter, Marianne."

"No, I assure you, I'm her only daughter and my name's Rachel. I was named after my grandmother, my mother's mother. I never knew her; she died in the war." She lowered her voice. "In a concentration camp. My mother never talks about it. She only mentioned it the once. Please never mention the war to my mother—it gives her nightmares."

I was quick to reassure her that I wouldn't.

"But as for a daughter named Marianne, I don't know where you got that from."

"My mother told me. She visited your mother in hospital when you were born."

Rachel smiled. "There must be some mistake. I was born at home in the front bedroom. My father, Lance, had died in a car accident not long before."

My face must have registered my surprise. Obviously, Rachel knew nothing about Grant or the real circumstances of her birth. Hazel had not wanted her to know about the trial.

I changed my mind about the visit.

"Evidently I've got things wrong. Do you know, I don't think I'll call on Hazel today. She may be tired. Will you be visiting tomorrow?"

"No—unfortunately, I can only manage it once a week. I'm a lawyer and always incredibly busy."

"Hazel must be so proud of you. She was a clever woman, your mother, you know."

She smiled. "Yes, I do know. Listen, you seem to be very fond of her, and you must have known my parents before I was born—would you like to come for a coffee, and perhaps you can tell me a bit about my mother's past? She never tells me anything. She's a bit of a mystery."

* * *

The café was shabby. We ate at a table with a broken plastic surface. The walls needed painting.

"Could you come and clean this table, please?" Rachel loudly demanded.

Other customers turned around. I cringed. The waitress appeared and sullenly slopped a grubby dishcloth over the surface. I wondered how many germs were cheerfully multiplying as we ate there. A bit of a come-down for a lawyer, I thought.

"This place has gone downhill," said Rachel, reading my thoughts.

We ordered two coffees. Mine was weak and milky, like the sort I'd always liked in the expresso bars of my youth. They call them lattes now, or cappuccinos. Rachel's was black and strong. We made some small talk.

"Did your parents know my mother well?"

"Oh yes. She lived two doors down—she was always in our house. She often confided things to my mother."

"What sort of things?" Rachel asked sharply.

"Oh, you know, about her early life. She used to have nightmares. My mother would comfort her and calm her down. She loved my mother, Marion. She told her she had named her baby after her, but she spelled it differently."

"Well, it didn't happen, I'm sorry. I've always been Rachel."

We drank our coffees. I spooned more sugar in—I didn't like bitter coffee.

"Tell me about my father."

"Well, as I recall, and from what my mother told me, everyone liked Lance. He was a big man, fair-haired, strong. Always willing to help anyone."

Rachel smiled. "It must have been hard for Mum when he died."

"Hazel was devastated."

We drank our coffee. My pulse racing, I asked, "Did your mother ever mention a man called Grant?"

"Grant? No. Who was he?"

I could not tell Hazel's secret. "Oh, just someone who lived in our street. He died, too."

"What, in the same accident?"

"Oh, no."

Rachel wasn't interested. "Did my mother know him well?"

"I think so. I think everyone knew him."

"She's never mentioned the name. Should she have?"

"Oh, no. I just thought—reminiscing about old times and that—his name might have cropped up."

"That's the thing—she never talks about the past to me. I know so little about her history, or that of my father. I would like to know."

She took out a lipstick and quickly rubbed it over her mouth, then put her lips together.

"How do you do that?"

"What?"

"Put lipstick on without looking in a mirror."

She smiled. "Practice." She got up and took her black leather handbag from the empty chair next to her. "Look, I have to go. It was nice meeting you. Those places—they're quite awful, aren't they? All those old biddies sleeping in their chairs all day. Not a job I could do, looking after them."

"Someone's got to do it."

"Yes, well. Not me. Still, it was the best place I could find. I think they treat Mum well. And she's still got all her marbles, which is one consolation."

"I thought she had Alzheimer's?"

"No, no, no, no. Sometimes she gets a bit confused, and sometimes she has bad dreams, but no, no Alzheimer's, thank God!"

"Oh."

"Look, I'll pay. I'll stand you this coffee as a way of thanking you for visiting my old mum."

"Oh, it's no trouble. No trouble at all."

But Rachel would brook no argument and I was talking to her back as she whisked away to the till. She waved a leather-gloved hand at me through the smeary window and then was gone.

I was left alone with my thoughts.

CHAPTER SEVEN

"They put these electric things on my head," Hazel said suddenly one day.

"What electric things?"

"I don't know. They made me jump."

"Oh."

"They gave me a gum shield so I wouldn't crack my teeth."

"Really?" This was news to me. It sounded like electric shock treatment.

"Was this before or after the trial, Hazel?"

"What trial?"

I did not pursue it. "Were you in hospital, Hazel?"

"I suppose I must have been. Did you visit me there?"

"No. I was just a schoolgirl, then."

She turned tearful eyes on me. "They took my baby away."

"When you were having the treatment?"

"What treatment?"

"When they put the electric things on your head, Hazel."

"What were they treating me for?"

"I don't know." I handed her a tissue. "Where did they take Rachel?"

"What? Has someone taken Rachel away?" She became agitated.

I was asking the wrong questions again. I consoled her. "Rachel is fine. No one's taken her away."

She slumped in the armchair. "Why did you ask where they took her then?"

"I just… I don't know, Hazel."

Now I was getting as confused as the old girl. Maybe I shouldn't visit her so often. Maybe I should stop my visits altogether. I didn't want to upset her.

* * *

Hazel sat with a Welsh flannel blanket on her knees, looking through the window. She began talking almost as soon as I was through the door.

"I couldn't get into my room. They wouldn't give me the key."

"Perhaps they were cleaning it. You don't need a key, not usually, do you?"

"The hotel room," she explained irritably. "They wouldn't give me my key."

She was in another world.

"Why wouldn't they give it to you?" I put my hand on to the scratchy wool blanket covering her knees.

"I don't know. There was no one there at the reception desk. I rang the bell, but no one came. A voice came from the room behind and said, 'There's no one here'. I said, 'I can see that. May I have my key. Please.'

"'I'm at lunch', the voice said. 'You're too early. You can't have your key yet.'

"'I have a room booked in my name. I've stayed here before. I've come to collect my key and I want to get into my room.'

"'Well, you can't,' the voice said. 'You'll have to wait till the manager comes. I'm new, see. I have to follow the rules.' She came out of the room then. She was young and nervous and had brown curly hair to here." Hazel indicated her shoulders. "She was too fat for someone her age. She should have been slighter. She was carrying a half-eaten sandwich. I think she eats too much."

A knock at the door and Lesley came in, balancing a tray of tea and cakes against the door as she opened it. "Waitress service."

"I could have made tea, Lesley," I said, taking the tray from her and setting it down on the dresser. There was just enough room; the photographs took up a lot of space.

"Her kettle's blown its element. We'll have to get her a new one."

"Oh, well, thank you then. She's very chatty today."

"Oh yes. Very chatty, our Hazel sometimes. Aren't you, dear?"

Hazel did not respond.

When Lesley had gone, Hazel hissed, "I don't like that woman!"

"Why? Is she nasty to you?"

"No, no. But she's too nice. She's not my friend." She looked me in the eye. "Your mother was my friend. Marion."

It appeared that she was lucid and remembering things. "Do you know who I am, Hazel?"

"Yes. Siâni. Marion's daughter. You've grown up. Your hair is different—you used to have pigtails."

I laughed. "Many moons ago." I handed her a cup of tea. "What happened to Marianne, Hazel?"

The saucer trembled in her hands. I steadied it. "It's all right, I won't ask you again if it upsets you. You were talking about the hotel. The receptionist wouldn't give you the key."

But I got no more from Hazel that day. She clammed up completely. We drank our tea, ate our Welsh cakes. I remarked about the weather, asked after Rachel. And then I left.

I wondered about the hotel story. What was she referring to? Did she once live in a bed and breakfast? Did she and Lance once stay at an hotel? Did she and Grant have an affair before she married him? Was she already married to Lance? Hazel didn't seem the type to have an affair, but then you never really know where people were concerned.

What did we know about Hazel's life before she came to live in our street? Not a lot. Only what she'd told my mother about having had such a bad start to life. But she was a grown woman when we knew her.

* * *

I went to see a friend of mine, Pat, who was a

nurse. After a smashing tea of smoked salmon sandwiches and very naughty cream cakes, I was stuffed. We lounged on her sofa, chatting. I told her about Hazel and asked about dementia and Alzheimer's.

"Sometimes she has spells when she remembers things and she knows me and she knows her daughter, but other times she seems very confused."

My friend nodded.

"The thing is, Pat, she's not that old—early seventies. Some people are much fitter physically and mentally, but she seems to have aged rapidly."

"Dementia, especially Alzheimer's disease, can begin when one is relatively young. It surprises people, but even at our age, the signs can be there of the early stages."

"I sometimes get the feeling that she does remember things but blocks them out."

"It's usually the short-term memory that goes. People can still remember things from years ago. Did she experience a trauma in her life?"

"Oh yes. There was more than one."

"Then perhaps her brain *is* blocking them out, but they surface now and then."

I thought of all the traumas in Hazel's life. She had more reason than most to not want to remember things from her past. I began to sympathise with the old lady. Why should I pry?

***

The next time I visited Hazel, she smiled at me. Evidently, she had forgiven me for asking her too many questions. More than likely the dreams she related to me were snippets of memory all mixed up—snapshots of her past. They didn't make sense to me, and perhaps she didn't know herself what they all referred to. Some of them she must have understood, but I had not lived her life, so I couldn't understand what experiences she had endured.

On that occasion, she told me about her wedding but confused her second wedding with her first. She told me she wore a maroon-coloured dress.

"I was there!" I almost shouted. "I was your flower girl. You borrowed my maroon handbag."

"Did I?" She smiled. "A long time ago."

She told me about Lance's monster car.

"I remember it."

"He loved that car. But he had to get rid of it—it was too big."

We had a very pleasant hour together that day. Hazel had had her hair permed and was really happy. She complimented me on my new blouse. She talked about my parents; how good they'd been to her.

But the next time I called, Hazel was irritable. She accused me as soon as I entered her room. "You didn't unblock the drain!"

"Come again, Hazel? What drain?"

This was going to be one of her bad days. Something had upset her.

"We had to clear out the channel, but someone hadn't finished it. You could see it had only just been started. The bricks were clean. They hadn't been soiled by the rain and mud."

"Where was this channel leading to?"

"My friend and I were supposed to crawl through it and get to the other side. And we couldn't. Lance was cross, but only a bit. He never really got cross with me, you know. He said we'd have to get spades and dig it out quickly. All of us."

"What happened then?"

"I forget. I forget. The next bit's gone."

"All right, Hazel. Don't worry. It will come back."

Lesley brought in tea for us, and Hazel asked me to turn on her small television set. Rachel had bought it for her birthday.

"I didn't know it was your birthday, Hazel."

"It was last week, dear. You didn't come."

"I had a lot on last week. I should have sent you a card, Hazel. I know what I'll buy you—a new kettle."

Lesley shook her head. Later, when I left, she told me the element on Hazel's kettle had not burnt out. They had removed it in case Hazel scalded herself.

I wondered about Hazel's tale of the drain/channel. Was it some kind of tunnel? Was it an escape attempt from the concentration camp? But surely she would have been too young at the time to remember it? Obviously, she had mixed up her fond memories of Lance, perhaps with those of some good man she had met years ago. Perhaps her mother had told her of some botched attempt at an escape. When did her mother disappear from her life? I thought of what my mother had once said about early memories being stored as pictures. Sometimes these images reappear in dreams, and because there are no words, we cannot explain them. How long were memories stored inside the brain?

CHAPTER EIGHT

I did not go to visit Hazel for a while. Daniel, my son, came down with flu. Then I had it. Then Gerry. We were all left pretty weak. My limbs felt like lead weights.

The flu was doing the rounds in my small town. Even the GP had it, so a locum had to be called in. I hoped it had not spread to the old peoples' home; oldies are very susceptible to influenza. Perhaps they'd all had their jabs.

When I felt well enough to visit Hazel, I found her physical condition had deteriorated and she was very frail. The manager of the home told me the influenza had swept through and all but three of the residents had succumbed, despite their annual flu injections.

"This was a very virulent strain," she told me. "Two of our most elderly residents died."

No wonder my family and I had been laid so low.

"Hazel has a strong constitution," she said, "but the illness has taken its toll on her."

Hazel's carer, Lesley, met me outside her room. "She's up and sitting in her chair, but don't stay too long." Then she took me in.

"I want to go outside," Hazel said as soon as she saw us.

"Not today, Hazel," Lesley replied. "It's a bit nippy, but in a few days if the wind drops and the sun shines, I'll take you for a walk."

"I could do that," I suggested.

Hazel appeared to be sulking. Lesley left us to make a cup of tea.

"So," I said, sitting in the other armchair, "you had that flu bug. I did too. We were all ill in our house."

She didn't seem to be listening. Then she suddenly came to life, as it were.

"I had a dream this morning. I went to the street where I used to live. It was a nice street, about twenty to thirty houses on both sides of a short street. Modern. Dormer bungalows they were called. I asked a few people where Marion was. People shook their heads and said no Marion lived there. At the end of the street, I could see there was a new development, a lot of houses all the same. They looked like council houses. Some of the pavements were unmade, just the paths laid out, filled with rubble. It was going to be a huge estate.

"I wandered around, but not too far in. I was afraid of getting lost, so I went back to my old street. Some of the houses had been painted and had white or cream walls. I think they call it pebble-dashing. I opened the gate of where I used to live and walked up the path to the side door, then I took a few more steps and looked around the back of the house. Clothes flapped on the washing line. The garden, mostly laid to grass, looked familiar, but it was no longer mine. I was upset. Then I retraced my steps—I walked to the end of the street. In the last but one house, a young woman appeared from around the side.

"'Are you looking for Rachel?' she said. 'I'm Rachel. Come inside.

"'I have a parcel for you', she said. Suddenly, I was holding a large flat object wrapped in brown paper, like a picture.

"'They told me you didn't live here,' I muttered as I followed her into the spotlessly clean living room. Not a thing was out of place, but it was quite bare.

"Then I noticed two cots. No, they weren't cots. They were like those incubator things you find in hospitals. Only, the babies inside were fully clothed. The one was dressed in a yellow cable jumper and was not quite a year old. The other glass cabinet contained a younger child. They both lay down, long and straight. They had identical faces. The woman appeared at my elbow. 'They're both mine,' she laughed.

"Then I became aware of another child in a large cot on the other side of the room. He was about five or six and was standing up. He was dressed like the other child, in a yellow jumper. He saw me and made faces at me. Strange sounds came from his mouth—I guessed he could not speak. The woman had disappeared. I was left in the room with these three children. I didn't know what to do. I was filled with emotion and was very unhappy. I wanted to go home."

I listened intently as Hazel rambled, telling her story with many pauses.

Lesley brought in the tea. "Has she been telling you about her dream, Mrs Lewis?"

Hazel glared at her.

When Lesley had gone, I asked, "What do you think this dream meant, Hazel?"

She seemed deep in thought.

"Who were the babies, Hazel?"

She didn't answer. We drank our tea and ate our Garibaldi biscuits. Hazel seemed exhausted, and I took her cup from her. Before I left, I reminded her. "Next time I come, if it's fine, I'll take you for a walk."

I went to find Lesley in the day room. "She's very tired."

"Yes, I think I might put her to bed. It took me ages to get her up and about this morning. It's the flu—it weakens them."

Hazel had been trying to tell me something. She had been looking for Marion and had then found Rachel. And then the babies—were there two babies? Perhaps Marianne and Rachel were not the same person. But then, who was the third child?

I wondered what had happened to Hazel between the time that she had left our street and the time Mr Thomas had known her. I had assumed she'd left us and turned up in his village straight away. But he'd mentioned a child. Marianne would have been a babe in arms.

I had to find out what filled that gap in Hazel's

life. Was there another mystery or scandal to unearth? The street she had described was not Mr Thomas's, nor the one we had lived in—those were typical terraced streets of the old mining villages. Perhaps Hazel had moved somewhere else before she'd landed up in Sue's place.

* * *

"I had a dolly in a pram—no, a pushchair—and I got my sheet dirty. And the wheels of the pushchair were dirty. I knew I would get into trouble, so I tried to clean the wheels of the buggy with the sheet. And there was a green wheelbarrow. I put the sheet in there to wash it, but everything was dirty and muddy. I couldn't get them clean. And I knew I would get into awful trouble."

I waited. There was nothing more forthcoming. Hazel had relapsed into silence. Was this a dream? Or was it a memory, one more snapshot from her past?

"Were you a very little girl?" I asked.

There was nothing. We both gazed out of the window. The weather was changing. Autumn with its lovely colours was giving way to winter, and the late warm days of September had gone. October brought with it grey skies and a fresher feel to the air. I had taken Hazel out in her wheelchair twice. On one fine sunny day, I took her for a walk in Green Acres' grounds. The company's gardener was out, weeding the rose beds. Hazel enjoyed her walk. She was chatty and lucid, remarking on the autumnal colours of the trees and acers. She appreciated the beauty of the late summer flowers.

The second time, I took her out of the grounds and along the street as far as the local shop. But she became agitated when we passed through the gates and clutched her woollen blanket.

"Will we be able to get back in?" she asked in a quivery voice.

"Oh yes. Don't worry."

But she hadn't relaxed, so at the shop, I turned around and took her back to the home.

Once she was safely back in her room, I asked, "Does Rachel ever take you out for a walk, Hazel?"

"Who?"

"Rachel."

She seemed confused.

I handed her the photograph of Rachel in her graduation robes. "Rachel."

"Oh, Rachel."

She seemed far away. We drank our tea. I noticed her little bird-face was becoming even more lined. Her skin was pale and paper thin.

"Grant loved me."

I almost dropped my cup. She had remembered Grant! The cogs were turning.

"He loved me, but he was too obsessive."

I waited.

"He said horrible things about Lance." Her hands started shaking. The cup rattled in the saucer.

I took it from her. "What sort of thing?"

"That I should never have married him. He cheated on me. I should have left him. Everyone loved Lance, but they didn't know what he was really like. Grant said that he had been loyal to me. He had never loved anyone else. That he had always loved me."

I asked her gently, "Did Lance cheat on you?"

"No. Yes. I think he did. I don't know." She shook her head. "Grant confused me. I made up my mind to leave him, but I didn't know where to go. I tried to run away, but he caught me and then… and then… he died." She began to weep.

Oh God, what had I done? Was I responsible for her memories returning, things she had hidden deep inside her brain? Perhaps I had probed too far.

I pressed the buzzer for her carer.

CHAPTER NINE

I saw Hazel one more time. She told me about a man delivering large boxes. They were empty. I put that down to memories of moving. Then she told me she had bought bouquets of flowers for her husband—which husband, she did not reveal. They were tall flowers, she said. Her husband had arranged them in the tall vases, wide at the top, and then he had put them on the windowsill.

"It must have been a big windowsill," I remarked.

She gave me a filthy look. "The sun came in through the window. My husband was pleased with the flowers."

I wondered if she was talking about Lance's funeral.

"Marion was there," she announced.

"Marianne your daughter?"

"No, no. Marion—your mother."

"Oh."

She gave me a look as if I was the one with dementia.

* * *

The next time I went to Green Acres, Lesley met me in the foyer.

"I'm afraid you won't be able to see Hazel today," she said. "She had a bad night and she's quite exhausted. The doctor's been to see her, and he's given her something to calm her down. She must have rest. I'm sorry about that, but I know you'll understand."

"Yes. Yes. Of course."

I stood, unsure of what to do. I had already written my name in the visitors' book.

"Would you like a cup of tea? You could stay and talk to some of the other elderly folk."

There were easy chairs in the foyer, a couple of them occupied by ladies much older than Hazel. One had staring eyes and looked as if she had no teeth. The other was asleep.

"No, no, thank you. I'd better go. When she wakes up, will you tell her that Siân called? Siâni, Marion's daughter. She'll know who I am."

"Of course she will. You're Mrs Taylor's regular visitor; no one else calls except Rachel, her daughter, and she doesn't come as often these days."

"No?"

"I think she's very busy. She's a lawyer or a barrister, I believe. Very high up. She gets annoyed because just recently her mum hasn't recognised her. That's the pity of Alzheimer's."

"But I thought she didn't…"

"Have Alzheimer's. Oh, yes—It's been creeping along, getting steadily worse. Rachel won't have it, you know. Such a clever woman, she doesn't want to think of her mum with something like that."

"She's in denial?"

"She doesn't want to think her mum is losing her mind."

"But sometimes Hazel is very with it."

"Yes, it comes and goes. In patches."

"She has snapshots of her former life inside her brain?"

"But the images are mixed up. What she says doesn't always make sense."

"I'm trying to piece them together."

"Are you now, dear? Well, I'd best get on."

A thin, reedy voice was crying, "Nurse, nurse."

"Are you sure you wouldn't like a cup of tea?"

"No, really." I went towards the door, ready to press the button to release me into the outside world.

"Don't forget to sign out."

"What? Oh yes."

I did so and turned around. "Lesley, did she have nightmares last night?"

"Yes, I believe she did. I wasn't on shift. David said she called out in her sleep a lot."

"What were her nightmares about?"

"I really don't know. Is it significant?"

"I think they might be."

"You'll have to ask David. He comes in at six."

The thin, reedy voice called out again.

"Is there anything else?"

"No." I was glad to leave. I suddenly felt claustrophobic. This place was like a prison. I reached for the button.

***

I went home in a strange state of mind. When Gerry came home from work, he found me sitting in the dark.

"Why haven't you put the light on?" he asked, switching it on and making me screw my eyes up.

"I don't know. I wanted to think. I went to visit Hazel, but she'd had a bad night and they wouldn't let me see her. I came over funny there in the home. I don't know what happened; I felt quite faint."

Gerry sat down beside me heavily. "I don't know why you keep going to see that old woman."

"Because she was a close friend of my mother and awful things happened to her."

"But it always makes you unhappy."

"But apart from her daughter, I seem to be the only one who cares about her. I think she's trying to tell me something, but I don't know what. I want to find out what happened to her after she left our street. My mother tried to keep in touch with her and wrote to her. I think she had one reply when Hazel was waiting for her appeal to go through, but then after she moved, nothing. Zilch. So my mother gave up. If Hazel wanted to disappear, that was her business, and my parents didn't really blame her. I'm sure Hazel had further problems in her life. Mr Thomas told me she was a troubled soul. But it's all coming out in a haphazard way. Sometimes she remembers things, and sometimes she has dreams, which I'm trying to interpret."

"Why don't you ask her daughter?"

"She doesn't seem to know as much about her mother as I do."

Gerry sighed and rose from the sofa. "Well, I don't really know what business it is of yours. Let sleeping dogs lie. Have you started dinner yet? I could eat a horse, hooves and all. What are we having?"

I jumped up. I had forgotten to put the shepherd's pie in the oven.

*　*　*

The next day, I called at Green Acres to see if Hazel was better. She was not in the day room, so I walked down the corridor leading to her bedroom. Lesley saw me.

"Mrs Lewis!" she called.

"Yes?"

"Hazel had another dreadful night. They think she might have had a stroke. She's been taken to hospital."

"Oh no."

We walked back down the red-carpeted corridor together.

"She was screaming out, David said, and asking for her mother. She said the guard had taken her away. She was thrashing about and said everything was grey. There were iron gates and she could not get out. David was afraid she'd fall out of bed. It sounded like a terrible nightmare. Then she sort of collapsed and became unconscious. David called the doctor."

I nodded. "It was more than just a dream. Did you know about Hazel's early life?"

Lesley looked blank.

"She and her mother were in a concentration camp. They came to Britain at the end of the war."

"Poor woman. That explains a lot. I suppose she still remembers it?"

"Not all of it; she was too young. But maybe she has some memories and gets flashbacks when she's upset. And maybe her mother told her things."

"I see."

We had reached the glass entrance door.

"What hospital is she in?"

"The General. Geriatric ward. Do you know what happened to Hazel's mother?"

I shook my head. "I don't think she knew herself. When she came here, she was fostered by different families. She told my mother that she didn't speak English at first, so she could not remember much about those early days. Everything was a muddle. But people were kind to her when she was a child. She learned English, went to school and never saw her mother again. It's amazing she even remembers her at all."

"Poor woman."

It was all right, I felt, to reveal this part of Hazel's history now. People would sympathise. I would reveal no more to the carer.

"I wonder if you could find out what happened to her mother," mused Lesley. "There must be organisations that could help you research the

Jewish refugees that came here when the war was over."

That set me thinking.

CHAPTER TEN

I contacted a Jewish synagogue in Cardiff and made arrangements to see the rabbi. He listened to my story and said he would do what he could to help.

"What was the woman's name?"

"Hazel told me her name was Hannah Elizabeth Hezekiah. Her foster parents called her Hazel and the name stuck, but she must have been old enough to remember the name her mother gave her, either that or she saw a document with her full name on it. Her first foster parents were called Smith, I believe, but she always went by Hezekiah. Her mother's name was Rachel—I know it's quite a common Hebrew name. I don't know how or when Hazel came to Wales, or when she married Lance Taylor. Where she was before that, I don't know. She doesn't have a Valleys accent, but I suppose she could have lived in Cardiff."

"It's a tall order, but I'll see what I can do to help."

He smiled, and I liked the man. He could have washed his hands of the task I'd given him. He could have told me it would be like finding a needle in a haystack, but he hadn't. He knew it was important to me.

* * *

I caught a bus into the city and then another bus to the huge general teaching hospital. The bus took me right into the grounds. I dithered and finally found the main entrance. I was freezing cold, but my hands were sweating. I wondered why.

There was a large reception area. I had never been there before, and it was quite daunting.

I walked up to the desk. "I'm looking for someone who was brought in a few days ago from an old peoples' home in Cwmbach. Suspected stroke."

"Name?"

"I think she'll be under the name of Hazel Taylor."

The receptionist raised her painted eyebrows but said nothing, scrolling through lists on her computer screen.

"Geriatrics," she said eventually.

"Hm, where is that, please?"

She pointed a scarlet fingernail. "Follow the arrow and take the lift at the end of the corridor to the third floor, turn left and follow the arrow."

I gulped. I hated these rabbit warrens.

Sure to get lost, I started walking in the direction she'd indicated. As I waited for the lift to descend, my heart raced. What was I doing here? Perhaps Hazel would not recognise me if she'd suffered a stroke. She'd been confused enough before. Would she be paralysed? Would she be able to speak? Would her face be twisted? I wanted to run.

The lift doors opened and out stepped Rachel. I had not seen her since that chat in the dreary café. She and I did not have much in common. She was a lawyer and very clever. Well off. I had scraped through my exams at school, somehow did enough to get accepted for teacher training, had endured rows of sulking teenagers for ten years and then accepted I was no good at it anyway and packed it in. Now I was trying to make my way as a writer, but it was hard work. The first rejection letters had floored me. Gerry suggested I write some short stories for magazines, which were actually published, and I cried with joy. But I was still attempting to write that great blockbuster that would establish my name as a true author. Rachel had flourished in her chosen career and had reaped the financial benefits as well as the personal satisfaction of succeeding in her work. Our paths would never have crossed in the normal scheme of things.

I made to smile, a small smile of pity, I thought.

To my surprise, Rachel grabbed my arm. "What are you doing here?"

"I've come to see your mam. How is she?"

Rachel frogmarched me down the corridor back the way I had come. "Don't you think you've done enough damage?"

"I beg your pardon?"

"Asking my mother all those questions. Stirring up memories. Asking me if I was Marianne. My mother got so confused in the end she even asked me what my name was! Did I know what had happened to Rachel? All this nosing and prying! Before you started coming around, I could have a nice chat with her, ask her what she had been doing, what sort of day she'd had—then you came along asking all your nosy questions, and she started having strange dreams and nightmares, getting all confused. Just what is your game?"

"No game, Rachel. No ulterior motive, I assure you. It's just that... Look, can you let go of my arm? You're gripping me so hard I'm going to have a bruise there."

People walking past were staring at us. Rachel relaxed her grip on me, but she still had a face like thunder.

"Can we go somewhere and talk?" I asked.

We ended up back in the spacious entrance hall and found two red plastic chairs to sit on. I explained, once again, how I had known Hazel when I was a schoolgirl and that she'd been friendly with my mother, Marion. How when she'd been in trouble, she would run to my mother and tell her all her woes.

"What trouble?" Rachel narrowed her eyes.

She obviously knew nothing about Grant or the trial. She knew nothing about her mother's nocturnal wanderings. If Hazel had not revealed the facts about Grant to her daughter, how could I betray her? Rachel didn't even know the truth about her birth, did she?

"Well, she used to have these dreams—

nightmares. And she could talk to my mother about them." I took a deep breath. "And once she and Lance fell out…"

"What about?"

"He slept with another woman." There, I'd said it. Please forgive me, Hazel.

Rachel's eyes were wide with shock. "But I thought they were devoted to each other. She used to tell me he was the love of her life."

"Oh, he was, he was. It only happened the once. She was a flighty piece. He felt so guilty he confessed. Your mother was so upset, he packed his bags and left."

"But he came back?"

"Oh yes, he came back. And she welcomed him back with open arms. Everything was all right from then on."

"Are you sure?"

"Yes."

"I see. And then the accident?"

"Yes."

"Is there anything else I should know about my mother? Obviously, she wouldn't have told me about my dad cheating on her—it could have put him in a bad light in my eyes."

I swallowed. "No. And yes."

She opened the clasp of her expensive black leather bag. "I've so little to remember my father by."

She took out her purse, and there in the compartment for notes were two photographs. She removed them and showed me one. It was of a younger Hazel, possibly a teenager, but unmistakably Hazel, with her short, curly brown hair, her bright inquisitive eyes and sharp little nose.

"Oh, how young she looks!" I exclaimed. "I never knew her then."

Rachel looked at it sadly. "She was a student, but she dropped out of university. A bit silly really. But she said she met my dad and fell in love and she wanted to marry him."

I smiled. "Young love, eh? We do silly things when we're young, don't we?"

"Did you do silly things, Siân? I didn't."

No, I didn't suppose she had.

I thought of some of the scrapes I'd almost got into with young men and how, just by sheer luck really, I had managed not to get myself pregnant before I married Gerry.

"Yes, I did silly things," I confessed.

"The things I wonder about, and what mum has never told me, is how she met my dad and how, if she met him so young, it took them so long before they had me."

"Who knows?"

I didn't tell Rachel the story Hazel had told my mother about her visit to the contraceptive clinic. She had not really wanted children, she told my mother, but her embarrassment at the clinic and Lance's wish to start a family had changed her mind.

Then Rachel showed me the other photograph.

"I know so little about my father apart from

what you've told me. Although he doesn't seem such a big man in this. But this is all I have of him."

I almost dropped the photo. Rigid with shock, I stared into the face of Grant Chase.

I told Rachel I was feeling queasy and that I should get home. She gave me a lift, which was kind of her. I rode home on a heated seat in her new BMW and we parted, almost friends. She told me the stroke had left a little paralysis down Hazel's left arm, but other than that, she was functioning normally. However, although Hazel had spoken to the doctors and nurses, she had not spoken to Rachel, just nodded and shaken her head when Rachel asked her if she felt all right or if she needed a glass of water. In the end, Rachel had left, and Hazel had sighed, as if she was relieved.

CHAPTER ELEVEN

I decided I would not visit Hazel anymore. The old lady was coming to the end of her life. She could not or would not tell me any more—and as Gerry said, what business was it of mine? I had not made any progress with my novel for weeks. I had to shake off this obsession with Hazel and get my life back on track.

Then I started having dreams, vivid dreams. I was always running or walking very fast, trying to get somewhere in a hurry. In one I walked down a long, long road. I think it was somewhere near Fulham Palace. I caught a bus and when I got off, I looked up and saw a railway station on the right, high above my head. I was still hurrying, hurrying. I knew I must catch a train. I could see the railings, and vegetation clung to the walls below.

Then I was in a room and Chloe, my daughter, was urging me to do something. I was watching a television above the door, although it wasn't on. Chloe rushed forward and the brightly-coloured cotton rug slipped on the polished floor. She fell headlong. I was anxious. I looked at her bright blue stiletto heels and thought, *What is she doing there?*

She rose, not a mark on her. "Come on," she said. "What are you waiting for?"

I could only assume that it was Hazel I was looking for in my dreams and that there was something I had to do, something I had to find. Don't let anyone tell you that people don't dream in colour; my images were bright and as clear as day. Sometimes, when I woke, they seemed very real. And so detailed.

In another dream, the railway line was not in London. I was going to Barry Island. But always, I was rushing to find someone.

My God, was this what was happening to Hazel? If her short-term memory was declining, perhaps her long-term memory, stored away in pictures, was becoming more real to her but was getting muddled in her dreams. No wonder she seemed confused.

I could understand the rushing-to-find-someone part of my dreams. Subconsciously, even consciously, I knew that though Hazel was not old by today's standards, she was very frail and might not live long enough for me to find the answers to the things that puzzled me about her life.

"But why does the railway station figure so prominently?" I asked Gerry.

"The scene of Grant's death," he replied, chewing on his bacon.

"Of course!" I cried.

Gerry carried on nonchalantly eating his dinner. He could not understand why I was so excited. He could not understand why I needed to fill the gaps in Hazel's life.

"Everyone has secrets," he declared. "Leave the old lady alone with hers."

"Have you got any secrets from me?" I teased him.

"I may have," he teased me back.

***

Although I did not visit Hazel again, I phoned the hospital every day to ask about her. She was stable, I was told, and calm—no nightmares, no more screaming. I interpreted this as an indication that the doctors were keeping her sedated. I worked on my novel, changing my main character's name from Hazel to Harriet.

A few weeks later, I had a telephone call from the rabbi. He told me he had been in contact with the Board of Deputies of British Jews, which kept national archives and accessed the Jewish Communities and Records. He had found a Rachel who had arrived with her daughter, Hannah Elizabeth, but that Rachel's surname was Joseph. However, Hannah's (or Hazel's) age had tallied, and the woman had given her husband's name as Hezekiah. Hezekiah, who had been a fair few years older than Rachel, had been captured by the Nazis some years before his wife and daughter, who had been hidden for some time. Unfortunately, he had perished in the concentration camp. Rachel and Hannah had been sheltered by neighbours and were among the last intake of the camp.

Reports from the time of the Liberation said the Nazis knew that all was up, and the camp commandant had shot himself. There was complete chaos; some of the guards fled and some disguised themselves as inmates as the Allies came through the gates.

"I suppose Hazel must have found out something about all this, perhaps from her mother. Were there any attempts at escaping?"

"Pardon? Why?"

"Hazel had a dream about a drain."

"Ah."

"Sorry, I interrupted you."

"I think Hazel's lucky that she doesn't remember some of the worst things that happened there. She was very young, and either she was too young for them to register, or perhaps she was shielded by the adults."

"What happened to them after they came to Britain?"

"They were duly processed and registered and taken to a shelter, but Rachel had contracted TB in the camp. Her condition worsened, and she was taken to a sanatorium. Hannah was fostered out to one family and then to another."

"She says that time was a blur."

"Well, she *had* been separated from her mother and she couldn't speak English, possibly she didn't have much speech at all, so that is understandable."

"What happened to her mother?"

"I had to contact the health authorities, who

went through the records of the sanatoriums in and out of London, and they found the name of a Rachel Joseph that related to the time. Not only did this Rachel suffer from tuberculosis but she had psychiatric problems. She suffered from nightmares and became very confused."

"Oh no," I cried. "That could explain Hazel's mental state."

"So you think this could be the right Rachel?"

"I certainly do. Tell me, did they give her electric shock treatment?"

"I was coming to that. It appeared that this Rachel had a child and corresponded with her."

"Oh, it all fits. It fits. Hazel had a dream about someone putting electrodes on her head. Do you think Rachel told her about it?"

"She did receive treatment. To get back to where I was…"

"I'm sorry. I keep interrupting."

"Rachel recovered from the TB eventually, but she was very fragile physically, mentally too. She had nightmares and began having seizures. She did receive various treatments including counselling, oral medication and electroconvulsive therapy."

"Oh my God! Sorry, Rabbi."

"I've also been in touch with adoption agencies and social services. I discovered a Hannah Elizabeth Hezekiah who was fostered short-term with an elderly couple, but they could not cope with a toddler and asked for an older child. She was sent to another family short-term, and then she went to a Mr and Mrs Smith on a long-term arrangement. They were non-Jewish but had lost a daughter during the war and desperately wanted a little girl. They were anxious to foster a child who had experienced a bad start in life. It seemed the ideal placement. And that's it. That's as far as I've got. I believe the couple died a long time ago and they had no other children. Does this help you at all?"

"Oh, it does. It does. It makes sense of some of the things Hazel told me. I wonder why she never talks about her foster parents?"

"Yes, it is strange. She must remember them."

"Why do you think she started calling herself Hazel?"

"I don't know. Perhaps the daughter of her foster parents was named Hazel. Perhaps Hazel herself liked the name and when she was older wanted to forget her past."

"Mmm." I considered this. "What happened to Rachel?"

"I'm not sure. The records state that, after treatment, she was considered well enough to leave hospital, but she was still receiving medication for the seizures. Perhaps she needed it permanently, for the rest of her life."

"Do you think she was not allowed to have Hazel back? Or perhaps she decided that Hazel would have a better future with the foster parents?"

"I don't know. If you would like me to, I can try and find out where and when she died, and where she might be buried."

"You have been so helpful. I don't want to put you to any more inconvenience."

"I think it's important to you, isn't it?"

"It is. I would like it if you could find out. It's not really for me. I think it may be too late for Hazel, but if not for her, then for Rachel, her daughter."

CHAPTER TWELVE

My dreams were increasingly vivid, and Gerry told me I sometimes cried out in my sleep. Oh God, was I turning into Hazel? One I remember was of me visiting friends, John and Barbara. I had two little girls dressed in pink dresses with yellow spots. The younger one was only a toddler and became very tired. I cwtched her in a blanket on my lap and rocked her to sleep. When she was finally away, I removed her two fingers from her mouth and noticed that her face was grubby and needed a wash. Her hair, too, was lank and dull. Then I lay her on my friends' sofa and picked up my other daughter. She was about three or four years old, and she wanted a cwtch from me too. My friends were nice to her, but she was tired and cross. "My sister's the baby. She gets Mammy first," she said irritably. I took her in my arms and rocked her to sleep. Then I lay her alongside my other sleeping child, and instinctively, she put her arms around her sister.

"They've had so much fun running around and playing this week. I must give them baths and wash their hair tomorrow."

When I awoke, I sat up in bed and looked at my husband, still fast asleep beside me. The dream could have been about my own children—I had two daughters, Sarah and Chloe—but something inside me knew this dream was about Hazel.

Christmastime came, and I was reunited with Sarah and Chloe.

Sarah had graduated in history from Birmingham University that summer. She had stayed in Birmingham, had a job in a library and was living with her boyfriend in a flat. Chloe was in her second year at Bath, reading philosophy. I also had a son, Daniel, who was a primary school teacher and still lived at home. He was unmarried, although he had a sometime girlfriend. It all seemed very casual, and we wondered if the relationship would develop.

We all had a jolly time together, ate too much, drank too much, and I was sorry when my girls left us.

Happy in the bosom of my family, I had forgotten my quest.

Lonely without my girls, and with Gerry and Daniel back at work, my thoughts went back to Hazel. I began to make notes in an exercise book.

1. *Who were Hazel's foster parents? What happened to them? Why did she not ever mention them?*
2. *What happened to Hazel to make her leave college?*
3. *When and where did she meet Lance? Did she meet him in Cardiff? How had she come to be there?*
4. *The problem of Marianne and Rachel— could they be the same person or were*

they different women? If so, where was Marianne? Wouldn't Hazel's child have been a very young baby when she was known to Mr Thomas? Should I interview him again to find out the child's age at that time?

Gerry always accused me of being nosy. I guess I had always been an inquisitive person. As a youngster I was always asking my parents what they deemed to be difficult questions.

"How do you get to be pregnant, Mam?"

"Well." She put down the plates on the table. "You have to be married first."

"Why? Celia Jones wasn't married, and *she* had a baby."

"Reg!" my mother called. "Your dinner's ready. Now stop asking silly questions, Siâni, and get the knives and forks out!"

* * *

The phone rang. It was Saturday. Daniel was in the hall and answered it.

"It's for you, Mum," he called, entering the living room.

I took the phone from him.

"Siân? It's Rachel. I'm ringing to let you know that my mother died last night." She sounded composed.

"I'm so sorry, Rachel. I was very fond of your mother, and I had known her, of course, as a lively young woman. Did she go peacefully?"

There was a slight pause. "The hospital rang me and said she'd had another stroke and that I should get there quickly. By the time I arrived, she was fading. She could barely speak, but…"

I waited.

"Just before she went, she opened her eyes and called me Marianne."

I waited.

"I really don't understand this business about Marianne. Was that the name she gave me initially? Why did she change my name? Was it out of respect for my grandmother? Perhaps she didn't want to offend your mother, so she didn't tell her?"

"Perhaps, but then she didn't know my mother as well as she thought she did. Mam would not have been offended—she was a kindly soul and she would have understood."

I tried to visualise Rachel's face. What was she feeling now? I remembered how lost I had felt when my own mother died. I missed her dreadfully and felt that my main prop in life, my anchor, had gone, even though I still had my aunts and Granny. But Rachel didn't seem that close to Hazel.

She said she would let me know when the funeral arrangements had been made.

"I shall definitely be there," I promised, "to say goodbye to Hazel."

There was a catch in Rachel's voice as she made her goodbye. So, despite the stiff upper lip, she was human.

I put the phone back on its station in the hall. Now I would never solve some of the mysteries that surrounded Hazel's life. I would have to be content with what I knew of her when she lived two doors away from us in Cwm Terrace. Singing as she pegged out her washing. Sitting at our kitchen table, drinking tea with Marion, my mother. Waddling down the aisle in a maroon dress, holding her pretty little posy in front of her bump, my maroon handbag hanging on her arm so as not to offend me.

"Why didn't she carry a proper bouquet?" quavered skinny Miss Williams, the street's spinster.

"Why did she get married again in such an awful colour?" asked old Mrs Carter.

"I liked the colour." My mother rose to Hazel's defence in a minute. "And she's been married before, so couldn't get married in white, anyroad."

"Quite. Quite," said wise old Mrs Davies, who always sounded wiser than she really was, I know now.

I would have to be content with these snapshots of Hazel that I retained in my memory.

I told Gerry the news when he came home from the allotment.

"So now was not the time to tell her you've found her grandmother's grave?"

"No. I'll tell her later, after the funeral. And it wasn't me who found it, it was Rabbi Bloomberg. I think… I think, Gerry, I'd like to go and visit the grave myself before I tell her."

Gerry groaned. "This is like the search for the Holy Grail. You're only going to be disappointed. What is Rachel's grave going to tell you? Make up your mind; there are some things you're never going to know and perhaps *should never* know."

"Nevertheless…"

"You're incorrigible!"

* * *

Gerry is not a mean man, and he accompanied me to the Jewish cemetery in London where Rachel Senior had been laid to rest. As he had predicted, I was disappointed. What had I expected to find? It was just a bare stone with the briefest of inscriptions. Of course, Hebrews did not believe in monuments. I laid a wreath on Hazel's behalf, bowed my head for a few moments, and then Gerry and I walked back along the path in the early spring sunshine.

CHAPTER THIRTEEN

Not everyone wears black to funerals these days. It's only for symbolic effect that people in black stand around gravesides in films. It's usually raining, too, to symbolise the misery of the occasion. All the negativity of the event piled on for the viewer. I have been to funerals where the deceased had stipulated that people should not mourn and instead should wear brightly-coloured clothing to celebrate their life.

At Hazel's funeral, I wore my best wine woollen coat with black boots. It was dry but so cold I saw my breath before my face. Gerry, God bless him, came to support me, and I needed him there, for I must confess that I felt very emotional.

Rachel sat with her husband and two children in the front pew of the crematorium chapel. She was very pale and the whole family radiated solemnity, but there were no tears.

I was surprised at the size of the turnout. From the home, the manager came along with Hazel's two main carers, Lesley and David. There were some other carers I didn't know by name. I smiled at the rabbi; it was good of him to come. He said after all he had discovered about her and her mother, he felt a closeness to Hazel. There were other people I did not know; I wondered if they had been Hazel's neighbours before she went into Green Acres. Where had she last lived? I made a mental note to ask Rachel.

It was a humanist service. As Gerry and I sat waiting for the service to begin, I wondered what the celebrant, a plump lady with a rigid hairdo, would say. I looked at the coffin with its shiny surface. Surely there would be no mention of Grant Chase or the trial? I became afraid.

"I'm starting a headache," I whispered to Gerry. He squeezed my arm.

The celebrant rose from her chair. She smiled at everyone. She was undoubtedly a kindly sort, but I had a lump in my throat and my temple throbbed. *Please don't say that this is going to be a celebration of Hazel's life*, I thought. Hazel, who went through such trauma.

The lady celebrant issued greetings to the congregation and made her introductions. "Hazel Taylor died last Saturday. She had suffered a stroke which unfortunately left her devoid of speech, but if she could have spoken I know she would have told her beloved daughter, Rachel, how much she loved her and how proud she was of all she has achieved."

This was Hazel's funeral, not a time for praising Rachel! I must have made a little noise, because Gerry nudged me.

The celebrant continued, "Hazel would never have guessed that one day she would have a daughter who would do so well in life. Because Hazel, herself, had such a difficult start. Born to

Jewish parents, Rachel and Hezekiah, during the war, eventually she and both her parents were taken to a German concentration camp."

I heard some gasps from the congregation. Evidently this was not common knowledge.

"Although Hazel's father sadly died in the camp, luckily Hazel and her mother were interned at the very end of the war. They survived and were brought to England. We have found out that Rachel was seriously ill, however, and later died. Hazel was brought up by foster parents. She was a clever girl and went to university, but she never completed her degree. She moved around a lot as a young woman, but eventually married Lance Taylor and came to live in the Valleys." She paused. "Poor Hazel was left a widow when her beloved husband died in a car accident. She was just a young woman with a baby on the way…"

I held my breath.

"Hazel did her best to bring up her daughter well. She moved from the Valleys and finally ended up here in Cardiff, near to her daughter and grandchildren. After a fall, she was given a hip replacement and she became a little confused. Also, her eyesight had gradually deteriorated, and so she left her flat to become a resident of Green Acres."

I let out a sigh. Gerry glanced at me.

"The staff at Green Acres were very fond of her, and though her early life had been difficult and complicated, Hazel had three very happy years at Green Acres before she left this life."

So many gaps. Were there things left out deliberately? Had Rachel asked the celebrant not to mention certain things? Or did they not know? Had Hazel covered her tracks so well that they had no idea about Grant or the trial?

"Hazel was not a religious person, but she did have some favourite hymns," the smiling woman said. "Our first hymn is one of the very first that she learnt in Sunday School, she told Rachel, her daughter, and she had always liked it. So, please stand."

We all shuffled to our feet. She read out:

"When He cometh, when He cometh
To make up His jewels.
All His jewels, precious jewels,
His loved and His own.
Like the stars of the morning,
His bright crown adorning,
They shall shine in their beauty,
Bright gems for His crown.

He will gather, He will gather
The gems for His Kingdom,
All the pure ones, all the bright ones,
His loved and His own.
Like the stars of the morning,
His bright crown adorning,
They shall shine in their beauty,
Bright gems for His crown.

Little children, little children
Who love their Redeemer,
Are the jewels, precious jewels,
His loved and His own.
Like the stars of the morning,
His bright crown adorning,
They shall shine in their beauty,
Bright gems for His crown.

The celebrant read out all the words before we sang them. Not everyone knew the old hymn, and the singing by the small congregation was uncertain and poor, but I knew it from Sankey's *Sacred Songs and Solos* which we had used in Sunday School when I was a child, and I sang the familiar verses with gusto, singing for Hazel. It was only when I sang the third verse that I realised why the hymn had been a favourite of hers. As a child who had suffered upheaval in her early life, the thought of a caring divinity who especially loved her and thought she was precious must have comforted her.

After the hymn, Rachel stood next to the celebrant. I had never seen her so unsure of herself.

"I was never close to my mother as a child," she began. "She was a shy person who kept herself to herself." Her eyes caught mine. "I had the feeling she was a secretive person who had hidden herself away. Perhaps it was understandable, given that she had experienced early trauma. But I never once doubted her love for me, and I would not be the person I am today if she had not believed in me and coaxed and pushed me to make the best of myself.

"My mother did not believe in Heaven or the afterlife. She said that we only get one chance in life, and it is up to each individual to make the best of what comes his or her way. If tragedy befalls us, we must endure it, and if obstacles arise, we must surmount them. And this I believe she did. And those wise words of hers have always remained with me and helped me in the way I live my life."

My eyes filled with tears. Gerry squeezed my hand.

"Amongst my mother's effects," Rachel said, "I found some books of poetry, and she had marked some of her favourite ones. One of them was *Abou Ben Adhem and the Angel.*"

She proceeded to read out the poem. It was one I had learnt in my school days. Fancy that it was one of Hazel's favourites. It had always been one of mine.

Rachel closed the book of poems and addressed us. "I also found a notebook in which my mother had attempted some poetry of her own. They are quite simple but from the heart. I should like to read you one."

She paused; her husband handed her an exercise book and then sat back down.

"If I could live my life again,
how would I change it?
Would I ask my God for riches?
No, not I.

Would I ask my God for fame and glory?
No, not I.
What is the purpose of it all?
Does anybody know?
No, nor I.

"The only thing I know for certain,
deep down inside,
is that truth and love and friendship
is the mainspring of a good and happy life.
So, can I change my life the way it is?
No, not I.
But I can be a better person if I try.
So, I must try.

"Have love and you have everything;
don't try to reason why.
I'd such a lot of love to give,
but my life has been a lie.
I have loved and I have lost,
but must learn to love again.
Amen.
Amen."

Rachel bowed her head. I mirrored her, my eyes full of tears that almost blinded me.

Rachel looked up. She spoke again. "My mother was fond of children, particularly babies. I know that she wanted the very best for my children. She left us nothing in a material sense, but her love and wisdom will remain in our hearts forever." She sat down.

The celebrant rose from her chair and asked us to sing the second hymn on the sheet, "Calon Lan". I had always loved this hymn, and as I sang it with feeling, I wondered if Hazel knew the English translation, for its sentiments echoed some of those in her own poem.

As the singing drew to a close, the curtains moved across the coffin and I gave vent to my tears. *That's it, Hazel*, I thought. *Your life, and now a part of mine, gone forever*. I had not felt so emotional since I lost my own mother.

The celebrant, in lieu of a prayer, recited another of Hazel's favourite poems:

"They are not long, the weeping and the laughter,
Love and desire and hate;
I think they have no portion in us after
We pass the gate.

"They are not long, the days of wine and roses;
Out of a misty dream
Our path emerges for a while, then closes
Within a dream."

She paused. "Thank you, everyone, for coming to say goodbye to Hazel. Rachel would like you to join her at the Fairbrother Arms, where a buffet has been laid on."

A sweet piece of music played as we stood and slowly shuffled out of the chapel, Rachel and her family leading us out.

Outside in the cold air, a woman in a purple

coat and old-fashioned hat came up to me. "Hazel was always a bit strange, wasn't she?"

"I'm sorry. Do I know you?"

"Oh, come on, Siâni—it's me, Jeanette. I used to live down the end of Cwm Street."

If anyone could be considered strange it was Jeanette—and the rest of her family! I suddenly thought, *Oh dear God, she must know about Grant and the trial.*

"Jeanette… Jeanette…" I pretended to think hard.

"Hughes, that was. It's Whelan now. I remember playing with you in the stream down the bottom end. But we moved away just before I started secondary modern. You went to grammar, didn't you?"

I nodded. What was she going to come up with next?

"I moved not long after Hazel came there. I remember Lance's really long car. Whatever happened to Lance?"

Oh, thank God. She didn't know about Grant.

"He died."

"Poor Lance. He was a nice guy. I didn't think they had any children."

"She was pregnant when he died."

"Poor Hazel. But she was a bit strange—didn't you think so?"

"No. Not really."

She didn't detect the flat, dismissive tone in my voice and carried on. "I saw the announcement in *The Echo* and I thought, oh I used to know a lady called Hazel, so I came along and I saw you, so I knew it must be the same one."

Why wouldn't she go away?

"She was friendly with your folks, wasn't she?"

I nodded.

"I didn't know about the concentration camp. She must have been a Jew—I never realised that. Fancy that!"

Jeanette's family had been strict chapel—no dancing, no singing, no drinking, no fun. They thought anyone different was strange.

I closed my ears to her chatter and tried to drift away.

Gerry must have sensed my distress, for he grabbed my arm. "Come on, we've got to go."

"Well, fancy seeing you after all this time," said Jeanette in the hat. "All the best."

I smiled wanly and tried to look as if I wasn't desperate to leave her.

We didn't stay long at the buffet. I only went because I wanted to speak to the rabbi and tell him we'd visited Rachel Senior's grave. I spoke to Lesley and David, Hazel's carers, nodded to the ones I didn't know, and then went to find Gerry, who was having a pint at the bar and talking to a rotund man with florid features.

"You can't go without speaking to Rachel," Gerry told me.

I looked for her. She was in a conversation with the celebrant lady.

"Finish your pint. I'll be outside," I told Gerry.

I stood on the cobbled path, waiting for him.

Rachel joined me. She wore a long black boucle coat and a black and gold scarf, every inch the grieving daughter.

"I thought you'd gone," she said. "I wanted to talk to you."

"Did the rabbi tell you?" I asked.

"What?"

I realised he hadn't. "We found Rachel's grave. In London. If you'd like to visit it."

"I see." Her face displayed no emotion. "Still digging?"

I felt my hackles rise. "I asked him for Hazel's sake—I didn't know she would die before we could tell her." I lowered my voice. "For your sake, too, if you're interested."

We glared at each other. This was not the time to quarrel. What was with the two of us that we could not get on?

"There was something I wanted to give you," said Rachel.

"Oh."

Perhaps she was going to make me a gift of a piece of Hazel's jewellery, or an ornament, to remember her mother by. I didn't really need anything. I had my snatches of memory; they were enough.

"I haven't got it with me. Is it all right if I bring it over to your place sometime?"

"Fine."

She knew where I lived from when she had given me a lift home from the hospital.

Gerry came outside. He shivered. "God, it's

brass monkeys!" He shook Rachel's hand. "A lovely send-off for your mum. All the best." He shot me a look.

I moved forward and embraced Rachel. It was awkward, and we were both rather stiff. Then, "Well, goodbye, Rachel. Lovely spread. See you soon," and we left her to find our car.

CHAPTER FOURTEEN

I dreamed about a man in a thick khaki uniform with a big bristly moustache and a flat hat. A beret, I suppose. I didn't know who he was. I was afraid of him and tried to hide behind someone— my mother? But the man smiled, so I knew he had no evil intentions. He had uneven teeth, rather protruding. He reached for my hand, but I wouldn't give it to him.

I awoke, sweating, and made my way to the bathroom. Where had this dream come from? Was I remembering something that Hazel had once told me? Or was her spirit entering mine?

Rachel came to my house the very next day. I felt a little uncomfortable receiving her into my humble abode. It was a small house—okay for me, Gerry and Daniel, but with only the one living room and small kitchen downstairs and nowhere really to entertain guests if the family was around. Luckily, Rachel came in the afternoon when both the men were at work. I got out my best china—a wedding present from many moons ago—in her honour and put out a plate of chocolate biscuits on the coffee table. She sipped at her tea but left the biscuits.

After the formalities were over, Rachel opened her large, expensive black leather bag.

"I wanted to give you this before it slipped my mind and I put it away somewhere." She took out a large, flat parcel. "It was in among Mum's things. It's a photograph album, but apart from photos of my mum and dad, I don't know any of the other people in the snapshots. I thought you might know them. Would you like it?"

"Shall I?"

"Oh yes, by all means. I mean you to have it, but perhaps you could tell me who some of the people are—or were, rather, seeing as most of them would be dead by now."

Daniel was home early; his school was out at 3.30 pm. He came into the room, saw Rachel, smiled, said "Hi" and disappeared.

"Is that your son?" Rachel asked.

"Yes."

"Chip off the old block. Just like his dad," she remarked.

"Yes." Something stirred at the back of my mind as I unwrapped the parcel. The album's front cover was rather battered, and as I opened it, some of the photographs slid out of place inside.

I entered another world, another time.

A photograph of my mam and dad stared out at me, bringing tears to my eyes. Rarely did we ever take photos in my family. Mam and Dad were both shy. Neither of them owned a camera. I remembered Lance with a camera. He liked snapping when they weren't aware of him, creeping up on them. But this was a posed shot, on our front doorstep. Mam in her paisley pinny, smiling self-consciously. Dad in his braces, shirt sleeves rolled up. His trousers were creased and he didn't smile at the camera, possibly because he had been caught off-guard without his false teeth.

I pointed them out. "That's my mam and dad, Marion and Reg, on our front doorstep."

"I thought it might be. There's a few of them in here. Is this you?"

I had never seen this other me before. Pig-tailed and scruffy in my chunky sweater and jeans. I put my hand to my mouth. "Oh my God, what do I look like?" I was transported back to my early teens. No wonder it took me so long to net myself a regular boyfriend—I looked so awful!

"This, I think, is my mother," Rachel said.

Of course it was. Though much younger than I had known her, the face was just the same, just a little plumper, not quite so bird-like. But the same eyes, the same nose.

"Oh, you must have this," I told her.

"Don't worry. I made a copy. That's why it's loose."

Hazel stood in what must have been a back garden. The back of the house was pointed a light colour, possibly white or cream. Was this the place she recalled in her dream? She squinted at the camera, for it was a sunny day. There was a half-smile on her face. I wondered where the photo had been taken. Rachel had no idea.

"I've never seen this album before. I wish I had; I could have asked my mother who these people were. Here's my father—I made a copy of this one, too."

This was not the snapshot Rachel had taken out of her purse to show me. This was a much younger version of Grant Chase than I had known. How on earth did Rachel have this in her possession? Maybe when he and Hazel had married, he'd given her some photographs of himself in his youth. But where were the pictures of Lance? Surely Hazel had one or two? Maybe she destroyed them? But why keep those of Grant and not Lance?

Rachel had turned the page. "This seems to have been a wedding, but apart from my mother, I don't know anybody else. I suppose my mother was a bridesmaid. See, the women are wearing white frilly dresses—well, I presume they are white. You can't tell with old black and white photos."

Hazel hadn't been a bridesmaid to my knowledge. I recognised Lance Taylor in his wedding suit and, because I knew it was her wedding, I could see that Hazel wore a different headdress from the other girls. I remembered Hazel's dream of white frilly dresses and the desperate longing she had experienced in her dream.

"Mmm," I murmured.

"Do you know anyone in it?"

"I don't recognise any of those faces." I pointed to the women. "It would have been before I knew your mother." I hadn't exactly lied.

Rachel turned the pages. Wise old Mrs Davies, skinny Miss Williams the street's spinster, Mrs Carter, Jones the baker, Jones the post, Celia the unmarried mother and her parents from number twenty-four, Margie Philips who only had one arm, kids playing in the street—including me—more of my mother and father, even Hazel gazed out at me, captured forever by Lance's camera. Of course, that's why there weren't any of him—he was always the one behind the camera, taking the photographs.

How strange it was seeing these old snaps for the first time. A different world we lived in then. The pavements looked messy and dirty; they had probably been covered with a fine patina of coal dust. The few cars on the road looked old-fashioned. Children often played on the street and in the road in those days. We had long skipping ropes stretched from one side of the street to the other. If a stray motorcar came along, we simply dropped one end of the rope. We came in from play muddy and dirty with holes in our jumpers and scraped knees, and it was accepted, because that was kids for you. We never locked our doors; everybody knew everybody else. I almost wept for the world of yesterday.

"That's just nostalgia," Gerry told me that night when I showed him the album. "The world was not a better place. Don't forget it was not long after the Second World War. Everyone was skint, we'd had rationing for years, loads of men had been killed in the war, London and other big cities which had been bombarded by Hitler and reduced to rubble were still full of bombsites when we were children. It was hard. Nowadays, people are not short of anything. There's food for everyone—"

"Too much food; we're all fat."

"Speak for yourself."

"And everyone's houses are full of junk and clutter—things we do not need. We've all got so much stuff. Kids are spoiled. They have to have the latest computer, the newest game, designer clothes, both the home strip and the away strip of their favourite football team…."

"Well…"

"Is that good?"

"Not really, I know. But I'm just pointing out that some things have changed for the better."

"But it was a more innocent age, wasn't it?"

"Not everyone was innocent, Siân. You are seeing it from your perspective. You were a child. *You* were innocent."

I hugged the photograph album to my chest. I had really meant it when I told Rachel, *"Thank you so much for letting me have this. I shall treasure it."*

* * *

I took Rachel to her grandmother's grave. We had travelled by train, then taken the Tube and then a bus. I can't say I'd warmed to her, but she seemed unsure of herself throughout the journey and I rather took her under my wing. I had been to the cemetery before with Gerry, but I got a little lost and Rachel's lack of confidence and my lack of any sense of direction made her irritable with me. I laughed it off. I could get lost outside my own front door!

At the plain unadorned stone, we stopped. I watched her face. Surprise, sadness and perhaps even disappointment flitted across her features. She read the basic inscription, lay the small, by then wilting, posy and closed her eyes. Was she praying? I stood silently at her side for a few moments. Then she looked up and faced me. Her face froze into the mask I had tried so hard to remove.

"Right. Let's go."

All the uncertainty, the fear of the unknown, had gone and she took charge of me, as was her usual way.

We spent much of the return journey to South Wales in silence. Then, on the last leg as it were, she asked me, "What else did you and Rabbi Bloomberg uncover?"

I told her that her grandfather, Hezekiah, had died in the concentration camp. It wasn't known how he met his end—perhaps the rabbi had wanted to spare Hazel the details—but he had been very ill anyway and Rachel's last recollection of him had been as an emaciated, weak old man. The men and women had been separated in the camp, but Rachel had seen him once from a distance. There was no record of him as a survivor, so one could only guess that he was one of the many bodies the Allies had found. Those that had not already been disposed of had been piled up in mass graves.

Rachel shuddered and looked pale. "And my grandmother. How did she die?"

"She *did* survive, along with Hazel, but on their arrival in Britain, a medical examination revealed that she had tuberculosis and she was sent to a sanatorium. Hazel—Hannah Elizabeth, she was then—was free of the disease and was fostered. Unfortunately, records have been lost; it appears they were damaged by fire, so we have an incomplete picture of those early years. At some point, Hannah became Hazel. Her last foster parents were recorded as a Mr and Mrs Smith. They are both dead now, and once again, there are no records of when she left them or where she went to. We could make further enquiries."

Rachel made no comment. We sat in silence again. I was beginning to get hungry. It had been a long day and a long time since breakfast. Rachel had not wanted to eat out, declaring that "London prices are ridiculous." I wished I had brought sandwiches.

"Did Rachel die from TB?" she suddenly said.

"She eventually recovered and was released from the sanatorium, but by that time, she was suffering from convulsions and her mental state had deteriorated. She had treatments but was not allowed to have Hazel back. Apparently, she signed herself out of hospital and just disappeared. Went off the radar completely."

"How strange."

"Perhaps her mental health meant she was confused. Rabbi Bloomberg contacted the Board of Deputies of British Jews who keep the national archives and found a death certificate, so was able to find out where she was buried. And that's all I can tell you, I'm afraid."

"But she was not a British Jew," Rachel said thoughtfully.

"No, that's true. Maybe she became a British citizen. I don't know, but the name fits."

"Maybe it's not my grandmother after all."

I felt deflated.

Then she said grudgingly, "I suppose I must thank you. At least I know a little more about my mother now. Whenever I asked questions, she always changed the subject. And she and I were never close. I don't know why. Of course, she did her best for me, but she always had this air of 'don't ask questions'. 'I won't tell you anything you don't need to know.' I sometimes felt she shut herself off from me."

I pondered. Possibly this was why Rachel, herself, seemed a cold fish. By the time the train pulled into Cardiff Central, we had sort-of bonded. Never to be friends but accepting of each other's differences. She bought sandwiches from the buffet car, and we swapped when she found hers contained mayonnaise. We moaned about the coffee and we moaned about the weather, the rain streaking across the dirty windowpanes of the carriage.

Gerry met me at the station. Rachel declined his offer of a lift and took a taxi. We hugged, more warmly than the last time, and then we both went our separate ways.

CHAPTER FIFTEEN

An official-looking letter came by post. I gathered that morning's mail from the doormat and took it into the kitchen. So much junk mail! I put those aside to be recycled. There were a couple of things for Gerry, one looked like an A.A. membership renewal form, some were bills. There was a clothes catalogue for me and this official-looking letter. I turned over the envelope: James, Jenkins and Paget Solicitors. A solicitor's letter! What could that be about? It was definitely my name in the window, not Gerry's.

A strange fear gripped me. Was someone suing me for something I had written in my last published story? I was always so careful to check my facts and went through my stories with a fine-tooth comb in case I had inadvertently written something incriminating.

I realised I was sweating. With trembling fingers, I ripped open the envelope. It was worse than learning your exam results.

Dear Mrs. Lewis, I read.

The letter was short, written in the usual formal style.

Following the death of Mrs Hazel Taylor, resident of Green Acres Home for the Elderly, Cardiff, I am bound to inform you that our offices are in possession of a parcel which she left with us some years ago. It was her wish that on her demise this parcel should be delivered to a Mrs Marion Watkins of 15 Cwm Terrace, Aberbach. In the event of Mrs Watkins predeceasing Mrs Taylor, the parcel should then be passed on to the daughter of Mrs Watkins, viz. a Miss Siân Watkins.

Following our searches, we have ascertained that you are the said Miss Siân Watkins, now with the married name of Mrs Siân Lewis.

In accordance with the deceased's wishes, therefore, the parcel now belongs to you. Please make arrangements to attend our offices to collect the said parcel, at your convenience.

Yours faithfully,

[Squiggle]

P. D. James [and a string of abbreviations]."

This was a month after Hazel's death. Obviously, the solicitor had tracked me down through the home, the undertaker, or even Rachel.

My hands stopped trembling. I was intrigued.

Later that day, I received a call from Rachel.

"I understand you've had a letter from James, Jenkins and Paget Solicitors," she almost spat down the phone.

"Yes, I've no idea what it's about."

"I've been in touch with them about my mother's will. There was nothing—zilch—for me or my children, but apparently she left something for your mother."

"Apparently." I became very wary. "Perhaps it's another photo album." I tried to placate her.

She snorted. "You do know my mother had virtually nothing when she died. If she's left you jewellery, then that really should come to me."

My hackles rose. "Whatever it is, Hazel wanted my mother to have it, Rachel, perhaps just as a memento."

"I can't get you out of my hair, can I? You're always there somewhere, lurking in the background. My mother left me nothing in her will. Why should she leave something specifically to your mother?"

"I don't know, Rachel. I really don't know. All I know is she was often in our house and she valued my mother's friendship."

"I gave you the photo album—isn't that enough? I shall want to know what she's left you. If it's anything valuable, it should really come to me. I'm her only child. And if it *is* anything valuable and you insist on keeping it, I'm warning you I shall contest it in court!"

"Rachel, I'm ending this conversation!"

Wearily I put the phone down. *Oh, Hazel, you are really making things difficult for me.*

"She can't do that, can she?" I asked Gerry at dinnertime.

Daniel was upstairs. The thump-thump of music came from the back bedroom. What was it with young men and loud music?

Gerry chewed on his lamb chop. "Dunno. I suppose it all depends on what's in the parcel. I doubt if the old dear had anything valuable to leave to anyone. If she left your mam what she considered her treasured possessions—her wedding ring, old photos of Lance and your parents—what would be the point of Rachel taking you to court for that? That would be stupid. No judge would proceed for that."

I chased my food around my plate. Daniel's music was giving me a headache. Gerry didn't seem to notice.

After more chewing, he continued, "She's a solicitor herself; she'd know it wouldn't wash. She's just threatening you."

"Do you think?"

* * *

I took my birth certificate with me to the office of James, Jenkins and Paget, just in case they needed any documents to prove my identity. I needn't have worried. I gave my name to the receptionist, who directed me to a waiting room. A young couple were sitting there, looking nervous. I wished that Gerry could have accompanied me, but he said he had a lot of work on and I was a big girl and could do this on my own.

I picked up a magazine on architecture and flicked through it, trying to look more composed than I felt. I put the magazine down. There were no interesting gossip rags, so I walked around the room studying the paintings on the wall. My fidgeting seemed to make the young couple more nervous. She, in a deep pink suit, and he, in brown corduroy trousers, were then called into another room. I sat down and tried to relax.

A tall, sixtyish, imposing figure of a man came in and said my name. "Mrs Lewis? I'm Perry James. Won't you come in?"

He shook my hand and opened the door to another room. I followed him in. The white-haired, rather quite handsome man invited me to sit, then sat down behind a large mahogany desk.

He smiled. "We have been Mrs Taylor's solicitors for some time. She left a parcel in our safekeeping long before she entered the home. Later, she made her will with us. A very modest, straightforward will, leaving most of her personal effects and whatever amount of money she had left to her daughter, Rachel, which I understand wasn't much. Later, she remembered the parcel and a codicil was added to her will, asking specifically that the parcel be left to your mother, and in the event of her death, to you.

"By the way, I forget my manners. Would you like coffee or tea?"

"No thanks."

He nodded as if I had made the right decision. "I understand your mother died a while ago."

I nodded. "Three, four years ago, now. My dad went first and my mother not long after."

He nodded. "Often the way. Often the way."

"Do you know what is in the parcel?"

"No idea. It was wrapped up with a note on the top, and that's the way it's been kept."

"Is it usual for someone to leave such a thing in your care?"

"Not usual, no. People often leave things in bank vaults. But sometimes people do ask us to safeguard documents other than wills."

"Are these documents?"

"Could be some official letters, certificates, things like that in the parcel. I understand Mrs Taylor had a troubled past?"

"Yes." I was imagining birth certificates, adoption papers, other kinds of old records.

Mr James pressed a button on his telephone. "Mrs Andrews. Could you bring in the parcel for Mrs Lewis, please?"

The receptionist entered, holding a brown paper parcel tied up with string. Attached to it, underneath a blue ribbon, was a handwritten note. She handed it to me and left the room.

I had never seen Hazel's handwriting before. It was quite neat. I could feel there were a number of things inside the parcel—they felt like exercise books or notepads. Perhaps I had been right when I suggested to Rachel that Hazel had left my mother more old photograph albums.

"Do I have to sign for it?" I asked.

"No, that's not necessary."

"I've brought my birth certificate."

He smiled—he was really quite handsome for an older man—and shook his head. "That's not necessary. You *are* Mrs Siân Lewis?"

"Yes."

"Well, that's fine. It's all yours." He rose and shook my hand.

I crammed the brown paper package into my Tesco bag-for-life and stood up.

"Goodbye, Mr James, and thanks for everything."

I made my way to the door, but he got there first and opened it for me. "Not at all. My pleasure."

* * *

"You didn't bring it home in a Tesco bag!" teased Gerry.

"Well, I didn't know how big the parcel would be."

"I don't think Rachel would be too impressed with you bringing home Hazel's crown jewels in a Tesco bag! Have you opened it yet?"

"No."

I wanted to be on my own when I revealed what Hazel had thought so important to leave to Mam or me and what, evidently, she had not wanted to find its way into Rachel's hands.

CHAPTER SIXTEEN

I waited until the next day. Gerry was out fixing gas boilers, and Daniel was in school. I carried the parcel upstairs like a long-lost treasure and laid it on my bed. I undid the blue ribbon and read the note Hazel had tucked inside:

These documents I leave to my good and honest friend, Marion Watkins. In the event of Marion's death, I should like them passed on to her daughter, Siân Watkins, who may do as she wishes with them. These requests are also written down in my will.

I wanted to try and explain. I did not mean to hurt anyone.

Hazel Taylor (Hannah Elizabeth Hezekiah)

I cut the string, ripped off the Sellotape and removed from the brown paper two large notepads, a scrapbook and two folders. The notepads were full of Hazel's neat handwriting. I would read them later. Newspaper cuttings cluttered the scrapbook. I guessed what these would be about. One was an article in the local press about Lance's accident. Attached to this was the notice that had been placed in the Deaths column of the *South Wales Echo*. Both were yellow with age. The next cutting was a report of Grant's death; another told of the trial.

The last one confirmed the successful appeal of Hazel's sentence and her acquittal.

Memories of that time came flooding back to me. Obviously, Rachel had never been told about this part of Hazel's life and Hazel wanted her to remain ignorant.

I placed the scrapbook back on the duvet and looked inside a folder containing loose photographs. Here was my childhood, returned to me again. Again, I looked at the faces of my parents. Here I was again in pigtails. This was how Hazel must have remembered us. I wondered if she was surprised at the present-day me when I turned up at the old folks' home. But she'd seemed to know who I was.

One of the photographs I had not seen before was of Hazel and Lance on their wedding day. She looked so happy I almost cried. Who would have guessed that such a tragedy would befall these two happy young people in such a short space of time?

There were no photographs of Grant. For some reason, although Rachel had been told that Lance was her father, she had been led to believe the photo of Grant she carried around in her purse was her dad. Why had Hazel muddled things up like that? Did she have no pictures of Lance other than those of her wedding? Well, why not show Rachel those? Was her eyesight so bad that she had made a mistake when she gave Rachel the snapshot? Or was Hazel so muddled by then that she had not known who Rachel's father was?

There were some photographs of babies and toddlers. I had no idea who they were; there were no names on the back. Were they of Hazel or Lance as babies? They were not all the same child. Was one a little Rachel? Could one be the missing Marianne? Rachel had told us all at the funeral that Hazel was very fond of babies and young children.

I put the snaps back into the folder. Maybe other things in this collection would reveal who the babies were.

I opened a blue-grey folder that tied at the front. Inside were letters. I quickly glanced through them. They were from Rachel, Hazel's mother, sent to her daughter via foster parents. I settled down on the bed to read them. The earlier letters were written in what I presumed to be German; I would need to have them translated. Later letters were written in poor English. After a brief greeting to John and Joan or Tom and Lucy, the words were directed to Hazel. Often she was addressed as "My dear, darling Hannah", or "My beautiful daughter, Hannah Elizabeth".

I smiled. My own mother never addressed me in such a way. British parents in the old days were never overly demonstrative in words or actions to their offspring. Love was understood; one didn't have to prove it by overt displays of affection. But what Hazel and her mother had been through in that camp! Rachel had lost her husband, and she obviously clung to her little girl. How awful it must have been when she came to these safe shores only to have her daughter taken away from her.

I read on. The letters were poignant. They spoke of Rachel's sorrow in not being able to provide a home for Hannah. They told of her wish for Hannah to be happy and well. In some of them, Rachel had not been able to find the right word in English and had interposed one in German. Hannah—or someone else, considering Hannah's young age—had put English translations underneath the words or sometimes in the margins.

The later letters still were in more fluent English. Obviously both Rachel and Hannah were becoming more proficient in the new language.

Rachel told her daughter that she had not been well and had spent a long time in hospital. She had not been able to see her in case Hannah caught the dreadful disease, but she was getting better, and when she was strong enough, she hoped to visit Hannah as soon as she could. I wondered whether that visit ever came about.

Then there was the saddest letter of all, which told of Rachel's nightmares and the treatments she had been receiving. She signed off by saying that, though her physical health was improving, she was "sick in her head"—her own words.

I cry as I write this letter. I know you are a good girl and that your foster parents are good people. They will take care of you and you will prosper. I know that you are speaking English well now. One day when you are older and my mind has recovered, we shall meet up and I know I will be so proud of my beautiful daughter, Hannah Elizabeth.

There were no more letters. There were no envelopes enclosed, so I could not find out where these were from or when. The creased, pale-blue lined notepaper with its faded writing was not dated.

I often get told that I am emotional, but I would defy anyone not to shed a tear after reading Rachel's letters. I found them heart-breaking.

I read them a few times and decided I would show them to Gerry. Perhaps he would agree with me that these could be given to Rachel, Hazel's daughter.

I decided to leave the large notepads for the next day. After quickly riffling through them, I saw they were diaries. Maybe I would now be able to fill in the gaps of Hazel's life.

I slept fitfully that night. First, I could not get to sleep at all. I kept thinking about Hazel and her mother. Then I woke up about two o'clock after dreaming: Hazel in her white wedding gown smiling, then Hazel in her purplish, maroon, too-tight dress. She was scowling. Grant was smiling alongside her. The material of the dress stretched as the baby inside her belly kept growing. And growing.

I woke. Too hot. I turned back the duvet. Just why had Hazel married Grant? She couldn't have loved him. Was it just to give the baby a father? Was she lonely after Lance died?

Then I needed to go to the bathroom. I woke Gerry up as I pattered back into the bedroom, and he grumbled as I got into bed.

"Sorry. Can't sleep," I mumbled.

I lay there, still, alongside my husband, willing sleep to come. I must have finally dropped off around five.

When I woke, it was light and Gerry was up. I looked at my bedside clock. God, it was half past eight. I grabbed my dressing gown and rushed across the landing.

"Daniel! Up." I knocked the door.

"Mum, I'm just finishing my breakfast," he shouted from below.

It appeared I was the only one who had overslept. I waited until my menfolk were out of the house, then ran upstairs to wash and dress. I could not wait to read Hazel's diaries.

CHAPTER SEVENTEEN

I took the parcel from the ottoman and removed the two A4 notepads. Numerals clearly marked them One and Two. I sat on the bed and opened Volume One.

The first few entries were dated 1951, about six years after the end of the Second World War. The writing was a schoolgirl's style, and reading through, I worked out she must have been about ten years old. She was very young to keep up a diary. As a teenager I had often started one, usually a bought one with a lock and key that never worked properly, and after a few entries I got bored or forgot or decided my life was too boring to write about anyway.

Hazel's notes were almost as poignant as her mother's letters. They described her foster parents John and Joan as kind and generous but quite old. Knowing young girls, I reckoned they could have been anything from forty onwards. This foster couple had lost a daughter called Hazel in the war and insisted on calling Hannah Hazel. I wondered if it was deliberate, so anxious were they to replace the lost child, or it could have just been a slip on their part. I often called my own daughters by the wrong names. Hazel/ Hannah enjoyed school and had made friends with the local children. She mentioned receiving her mother's letters and looked forward to seeing her when she became better.

I became sad as I read.

I waited today by the window for Mum but she did not come. I waited a long time until it was almost dark and then I knew that she wasn't going to come and see me. I was sorry. I wanted to show her some pictures I had drawn and a poem I had written. She never comes. She was supposed to have come last week but she didn't. Auntie Joan said she must be ill.

There were a few entries written in the same vein, but in one she was getting cross because of her mother's broken promises. Then her mother had evidently written to tell her about the fact she was having psychiatric treatment.

My mother is going loopy. She says she is "sick in the head". I hope it's not catching. I hope I don't lose my marbles when I am growing up. I think she has to go to a mental hospital. Asylums they are called. I don't want a mad mother.

I put down the notebook in sorrow. Poor Rachel. Hazel was only tiny when she and her mother were captured. She would perhaps have been hungry, frightened, confused, but she would not have been aware of all those dreadful things that happened at that terrible camp. Obviously, Rachel had been affected both physically and mentally, but at ten years old, Hazel could not have understood what the people there suffered or how it had affected her mother.

I went downstairs to make myself a cup of coffee and took it back up to read the next part of Hazel's diary. The writing had changed—it sloped more to the right—and the date was now 1954. Hazel would have been about thirteen.

I have been with Mr and Mrs Smith for nearly a year now. Uncle John and Auntie Joan said they were too old to look after me and then Uncle John had a heart attack, so I was sent here. Mr and Mrs Smith are called Tom and Lucy. They thought my name was Hazel because everyone calls me it. They were surprised to find my real name is Hannah but thought it would be easier if they stuck to Hazel. Less confusing that way, they said. I get fed up with correcting people and I couldn't care less anymore. Hannah or Hazel, it doesn't matter to me.

My mother doesn't write anymore. She was the only one who called me by my full name, Hannah Elizabeth. She is a Jew and her name is Rachel. I am Hazel Smith in school and that's all right because Auntie Lucy and Uncle Tom treat me as if I'm their own daughter. I have my own bedroom and I wanted it painted pretty and pink and Uncle Tom painted it for me. I have lots of toys and teddies, dolls and things, but really I'm too old for them. I've got a doll's house and a bike, and I like to ride on my bike. Aunty Lucy and Uncle Tom have got a big garden with fruit trees and vegetables and a shed. I am very happy here.

There were a few more entries like this. I began to skip through some of them. She wrote of trips to the seaside, to the cinema (like me, she called it 'the pictures'). She seemed a very happy, well-adjusted little girl. I saw no reason why I could not let Rachel have this diary.

There was no more mention of her mother. Perhaps, like adolescent girls worldwide, so much was going on in her world as she entered through the portals of womanhood that her mother's memory was becoming more distant and less important to her. Either that or she had just given up on seeing Rachel ever again.

Hazel wrote about her friends in school and in the neighbourhood and occasional spats she had with them. She wrote about 'old-fogey' teachers and 'boring lessons', much as I did when I was a teenager. She wrote about a handsome boy called Ronald. He lived just down the street from her and was about the same age.

Then something leaped out at me from the page. I had to put my mug down quickly on the bedside table. I read her words again.

I don't want to go into the shed with Uncle Tom. He makes me do disgusting things. He is a very kind man but he gets cross with me when I won't do them and says he will send me to a children's home if I refuse. I don't want to go to a children's home. I like it here.

Another entry read: *I must not tell Auntie Lucy what Uncle Tom is doing to me. She will be angry and she won't believe me. No one will believe me. They'll say I am making it up. I am so scared.*

After this, the same feelings resurfaced a few

times in her writing. It was obvious that Tom Smith was abusing Hazel sexually, and the girl was frightened and disgusted.

The entries became patchy and irregular. Then in one she described her birthday. She must have been fourteen. Tom and Lucy Smith had held a party for her, and she'd invited all her friends to her house, including the handsome Ronald. She split some orangeade on her blouse and went upstairs to change it. Below her, the new music called "Rock and Roll" blared from the gramophone. Her foster father followed her into the bedroom. No one heard Hazel's shouts. Though it was not actually described as such, what occurred there must have been rape.

I was shocked. Poor Hazel! In her safe haven she had been taken advantage of and abused. This was dreadful! I could not let her daughter read this. I would not reveal Hazel's dark secret.

This must have gone on for some time. In an entry written sometime later, Hazel wrote that she was afraid she could be pregnant. Oh my God— that man, that animal!

More extracts from Hazel's diary revealed a sad tale.

I am being taken away from here. I have to go into a special home for girls like me. Auntie Lucy is furious with me. She and the others are blaming Ronald. Poor Ronald. He has denied it but they don't believe him. I have denied it but they don't believe me either. We have only ever kissed and that was only twice. He has never even touched my breasts.

Auntie Lucy won't look at me. She has even stopped raging at me, saying I am ungrateful. To do this to them after all they've given me. She says she never wants me back. Uncle Tom never says anything. I can't tell Auntie Lucy the truth. She would never believe me.

I am to go from here tomorrow and I am scared, but in a way, I am glad I am going. I can't bear to see Uncle Tom's face. Everyone thinks he is such a nice man. Perhaps it's just as well if everyone thinks it was Ronald who 'defiled' me. Auntie Lucy could never bear the truth.

Hazel was told that her baby would be adopted. She was taken to a home for unmarried mothers, most of them in their late teens or early twenties. Hazel was the youngest one there.

The telephone rang. I could not find the upstairs handset, so I raced downstairs. It was one of those annoying cold calls from a call centre. I should have checked the number. I slammed down the handset and went into the kitchen to make myself a ham sandwich.

I could not stop thinking of poor Hazel's predicament. The poor girl, only a teenager, not much older than I had been when I met her, had been impregnated by her foster father. She could not tell anyone. He had got away with the most atrocious behaviour. The beast!

I took a tray upstairs to carry on reading.

CHAPTER EIGHTEEN

Hazel gave birth to a boy. Alone, except for a woman in a blue uniform. I assumed that was the midwife. Hazel had been in pain and screamed for her mother.

I suddenly remembered my mother's face even though I hadn't seen her for years. Where was she and why hadn't she come for me? The fat nurse slapped my face and told me to be quiet or I would frighten the other girls. She told me to quickly push the baby out. I didn't know it hurt so hard to have a baby. I looked at the ceiling. It was full of cracks. This was an awful place. I braced myself and pushed hard. Then I felt something slop out in a rush. I heard a baby cry. Someone else came into the room. I heard a man's voice.

There is something wrong with my baby. They told me I could not see him, but yesterday I went down the corridor and looked into the nursery. There were babies in cots. I think mine is the last in the row, by the wall. He has dark hair. They tell me that because he is not right, he will not be able to be adopted. He will have to go into a home for deformed children. Why did my baby have to be deformed? Is it because I did a sinful thing?

The other girls ask me what I am writing. I say

I am writing a letter to my friend, and I hide this notebook under my clothes.

Last night I dreamed I was with my mother in that place again. There were wire fences and big sheds and concrete blocks. Everything was grey and the people were grey. There was a horrible stench. My mother was in rags and she was crying. I woke up crying and I had a row from the nurse. I hate this place. I hate it, hate it. Today my friend Theresa left. She is going to live with her auntie in Cornwall. I wish I had an auntie in Cornwall. I have nowhere to go.

My throat hurt. I didn't hear him on the stairs. Suddenly the room was filled with light. It was an overcast, grey day, and I hadn't noticed the evening drawing on and the daylight fading fast.

"Hi, Mum. Why didn't you put the light on? What are you reading?"

I blinked and shut Hazel's diary. "Nothing, Dan. I forgot the time. What time is it?"

"Half four. I stayed on for football, but the rain started coming down in stair rods, so I packed the kids off home. What's for tea?"

My throat still felt constricted. "Curry," I managed.

"Great. Homemade?"

"Homemade. I'll get on to it now."

"And all the works—bhajis, samosas, poppadoms?"

"Yup."

"Good-oh." And he was gone.

I tucked the diary away in the ottoman under

some sheets and prepared to become a mam again.

"Where did you sling your muddy boots?" I called as I made my way downstairs.

"In the utility room," he shouted back. "They're not too bad. I scraped most of the mud off."

In my youth we had a scullery where we did all the washing—the dishes, our clothes, ourselves—not a "utility" room. I smiled to myself as I recalled my brother, ten years older than me, coming home with his dirty football kit and my mother fussing and complaining. I didn't complain with Daniel. He was not a bad bloke, and one day he would be gone from home, and how I would miss him!

* * *

After Dan had gone to bed, Gerry and I watched television for a bit, but there was not much on after half past ten. Gerry switched the telly off and went into the kitchen to make a cup of tea. I followed him in and told him what I had read in the diary. He was quite shocked.

Now, Gerry is quite a placid man who takes what life throws at him with a calmness that sometimes annoys me. When life throws stuff at me, I throw it back. But Gerry is philosophical, rational and slow to anger. For him to display shock was unusual.

The phone rang. I picked up. It was Sarah.

"Mum, I'm sorry it's so late. Do you think I

can come home this weekend? I've got a few days off, and I haven't seen you and Dad since Christmas. Oh, and Warren's not working this weekend either, so he'd like to come as well."

How could I say no to my daughter? I missed both of my daughters, but as a student, Chloe came home more frequently than her sister. Warren was Sarah's boyfriend; they lived together in Birmingham and supposedly were saving up to get married. He was a nice boy, but he rarely went home to see his own parents and often came to stay with us. Sarah knew my rules.

"You can stay in Chloe's bedroom. I'll just run the hoover around. Warren can sleep with Dan in his room. I'll put up the camp bed."

Sarah chuckled. "You're so old-fashioned, Mum."

"Them's the rules, chick."

"I know, I know. See you then."

And she was gone. Blast, now I wouldn't be able to read through the rest of Hazel's diaries over the weekend.

***

They arrived on Friday ravenous, so we ordered pizzas from Dominos, and we chatted until the early hours of Saturday morning. Everyone had a lie-in on Saturday except me. I lay awake listening to the raucous din of the early morning that some people call "the dawn chorus" and decided at seven o'clock to go downstairs and have breakfast.

I had only managed a quick dip into the diary on Thursday and found the entries after the birth of Hazel's baby ended abruptly. She spoke of her wish to name the baby after her father, but she could not remember his name. She thought it might have been Joseph. If she'd known where her mother was, she could have asked her, but Rachel had disappeared and Hazel did not know how to contact her. If she could find her, she would not tell her about the baby.

The authorities had taken little Joseph away and didn't say where he had gone. Hazel never got to hold her child. She never got to see his face properly. What was so wrong with him? Was his face deformed? Or was it his limbs? She was extremely upset.

I turned over a few blank pages. Then I saw some more writing. These entries were dated 1958 and the hand was more mature, much more like that of the note attached to the parcel. I decided to read these when Sarah returned to Birmingham.

* * *

Saturday night was football night, and while the three male members of the family slouched on the settee watching the telly, Sarah and I were washing up after a late supper. Sarah was up to her elbows in suds and I was wiping, stacking and putting away.

"When are you going to invest in a dishwasher?" she moaned.

I gestured around my tiny kitchen. "And where would I put it?"

"Outside in the shed?"

The word 'shed' had an effect on me. I put down the plate I was wiping.

"Mum, what's wrong?"

"Nothing." I picked up another plate.

She turned around and waved her soapy Marigolds at me. "You've been acting strange this weekend. You seem very distracted. Is everything all right with you and Dad?"

I blinked. "Yes. We're fine. I think."

"Stop it! You always add that on at the end. No, really." She plunged her hands back into the water. "You must tell me if there's something up. Don't leave me in the dark."

The football match was ninety minutes long. The programme had been running for ten, so that left eighty more minutes, plus the half-time interval, plus the after-match analysis from the pundits. I had plenty of time to tell her.

I took a deep breath.

CHAPTER NINETEEN

"Do you remember a woman I told you about? Her name was Hazel."

"Yes. You went to her funeral with Dad."

I put down my teacloth and sat on a stool. Out it all poured. Apart from when we made a cup of tea for the boys at half time, I sat and told her the whole of Hazel's sad story.

"Can I see the diaries?"

"Not yet—I want to finish reading them first. I want to fill in the gaps of her life and then perhaps I'll understand more about her, the reasons why she did what she did, the meaning of her dreams, and solve the mystery of Marianne/Rachel."

"Perhaps she just changed the child's name. People do sometimes. Even *her* name was changed from Hannah to Hazel."

"Perhaps. But there's a discrepancy I don't understand. When she left prison, her baby—Marianne—was a babe in arms. Mr Thomas, who I went to see in Thomastown where she went to live, remembers her with a little girl. Now either that baby had magical qualities and aged extremely fast, or Hazel had another child. It doesn't fit."

We heard a loud cheering from the living room. I took Sarah upstairs and showed her Rachel's letters, the newspaper clippings and the folder of photographs. This was all a new world to her. And an old world. All in the past. She had been a student of history, but of times long since; recent history of the world I grew up in had never really interested her. I had told her about the mining villages, but the mines had gone many years ago. She and her sister could not envisage a time when collieries and all the outbuildings— the winding gear, the 'buckets' suspended high above us, huge black coal tips—dominated our landscape, how the people themselves were so full of life and vigour. The air may have been full of soot and smuts, but I was such a happy child, and all the children that I played with were happy too. They were boisterous and lively, full of fun.

I had told her about washing in tin baths in front of the fire; of using an outside toilet, which would be freezing on a winter's day; of Jack Frost patterns on the *inside* of the windowpanes; washing clothes by hand in a tub with a washboard. She had smiled at me indulgently. She had grown up with televisions, record players, CDs, Walkmans, videos and then DVDs, computers and computer games, the internet, everybody owning washing machines, dishwashers, tumble driers, every household with a car, or even more than one car. How the world had moved on! From vinyl records to tapes, to CDs, and now downloading—what was that? From telephones with separate handsets and having to dial a number with a spinning disc, to cordless phones, to digital touch-tone keypads, answer phones, and finally to mobiles that include cameras, play tunes and apps—whatever those were. I used to write letters, then sent faxes, then there was texting and emails. How everything had changed during my lifetime. I could not keep up with the changes and could no longer operate my DVD with its timer or tune in my television with its multiple channels, so I relied on Gerry or Daniel to do it. I got confused with desktops, laptops, notepads, iPads, iPhones, Wi-Fi; could not get my head around Facebook, Facetime, Twitter, blogs and all the other computer stuff. It seemed I barely had time to turn around before a new invention came into use. Sarah could not think of a world without these modern things. She could not really visualise a world like the one I had grown up in.

But she *was* interested in Rachel's letters. She was a woman, after all, and other people's personal lives were intriguing to her.

She became quite sad. "So, what do you think happened to Rachel?"

I shrugged. "When she left the sanatorium, she was on medication for mental problems and she started having fits. Perhaps she got depressed, perhaps she stopped taking her tablets. But when she died, somebody knew who she was and buried her properly."

Sarah was thoughtful. "If her mental state deteriorated, perhaps she was sectioned under the Mental Health Act. Perhaps the authorities thought it better not to inform Hazel of this as she was too young."

"In that case, then, there was no mysterious disappearance of the mother. Rather, Hazel was simply kept from knowing the truth. But I don't know—don't you think at some stage Hazel should have been told?"

"Maybe," Sarah pondered. "But don't forget Hazel had other things to worry about—with the early pregnancy and removal from the foster home where she had been so happy at first."

"In that case then, social services would perhaps have thought she might not have been able to cope with the knowledge that her mother was in an asylum."

"Mind you, she does mention her mother going into an asylum, you said. So, I think she knew but didn't want to acknowledge it."

"You're probably right. So, she might just have been in denial."

"Later on, perhaps she felt guilty, so she decided to change the baby's name to Rachel."

"I'm still not sure about that."

To cheer Sarah up, I showed her the photographs. She laughed at the sight of me in my pigtails and asked if she could keep the one of her grandparents, Marion and Reg. I told her I'd make copies for her and Chloe. Dan could have the original when I died.

She shuddered. "Don't talk like that!"

She sifted through the photos and laid down the ones of the babies.

"One of these could be Joseph."

"No. She writes that she never saw him properly. They whisked the babies away quickly in those places. They didn't want the young women to get too attached to them."

"How cruel."

"Yes, but back then I suppose they thought it was for the best. What would Hazel have done at fourteen with such a tiny baby? She had no home, no mother to help her. And they told her there was something wrong with the child. How would she have coped?"

"These days social services would have helped her."

"Pish. Think of all the babies and children who suffer today even though we have social services to help people! And look how Hazel was abused by the people who were supposed to care for her!"

Sarah sighed. "Read the rest, Mum, and let me know what happens to her next."

"I will. And then I might ask you to help me decide what to do with the diaries."

"Burn them."

"Do you think?"

"Hey, you two!" Gerry called up. "Have you both gone to bed?"

I put the parcel back into the ottoman.

* * *

The next day being Sunday, Gerry made us all a huge fry-up breakfast, and the four of us tucked into bacon, sausages, tomatoes, eggs and fried bread. Daniel was dead to the world as usual. Gerry took the frying pan to the bottom of the stairs and waved it about, wafting the delicious aroma towards his lazy son.

The telephone rang.

Sarah picked up. "Who is this?"

Pause.

"Sarah."

Pause.

"I beg your pardon?"

Pause.

"No."

Pause.

"You've got a bloody cheek."

Pause.

"Nothing like that. Only old photographs and letters."

Pause.

"And the same to you too." She pressed the off button.

I raised my eyebrows enquiringly. "Rachel, Hazel's daughter, I guess?"

"You guessed right. What a rude woman! You can guess what she wanted."

"She thinks her mother's left me a family heirloom or something. What a surprise she'd have if she knew."

CHAPTER TWENTY

There were very few entries left in the first diary. One, from 1959, told of Hazel's thrill at being accepted into Leeds University to study English literature. I wondered how she had got that far. After her baby was born, where did she go? Where did she study? I began to build up respect for the young Hazel, so far removed from the prematurely old lady in Green Acres with a confused mind. After all she had been through, she was able to concentrate on her lessons enough to pass exams to go to university.

Where had she found a roof over her head? Presumably, after the Smiths had turned their backs on her, she was fostered by another couple or sent to a children's home as she had feared. Some of these places could be full of difficult, sometimes rowdy, youngsters, their behaviour often caused by the problems they had suffered at their own homes—sometimes by parents who were negligent or abusive, who were drunks or drug addicts. It was no wonder that such children became withdrawn or went the other way and became angry, displaying violent tendencies. Somehow Hazel had found enough peace and quiet to carry on with her homework. Perhaps she would explain more in the next notebook.

Hazel sounded like a typical student, full of life and excited at the prospect of attending new surroundings and meeting new, interesting people. Her diary entries became short and sporadic—evidently, she was going out to parties, enjoying herself as well as studying, and far too busy to want to record her life. I found no mention of her mother, her foster parents, the baby Joseph or anything of her former woes. Either she had purposely blocked out those memories or the bad things had simply faded as her life improved. She had decided to grasp this opportunity with both hands and, as they say today, move on.

In the last few entries, I got a picture of how much she was enjoying her new freedom and friendships. She visited other students' homes and stayed with them when the university closed for summer recess. She spoke of going to the races and she and her friend wearing straw bonnets. They had no money but loved the dressing-up part of it and mixing with the crowds. She told of staying up till the 'wee small hours' discussing favourite authors—hers were Thomas Hardy and George Eliot. She enjoyed the poetry of Tennyson, T. S. Eliot, Hardy and Byron. She was even trying her hand at composing some verses herself. Shakespeare was a revelation to her, having struggled with his plays for her A-level. Suddenly, she could understand and appreciate what he was trying to convey and on more than one level.

Tales of getting 'squiffy' revealed that, even then, students got drunk and embarrassing at times. I was delighted that Hazel was having such fun. Various names appeared in her notes: Johnny A, Big Fred, Jenny, Jean and Sylvia. Then one name jumped out at me from the page—Grant. Was this the same Grant that I had known, Grant Chase? I felt cold.

The telephone rang. I decided to ignore it. I had to find out about this man.

She wrote about going on a date with Grant. She liked him, but he was very possessive and became jealous if she smiled at other boys. She liked him quite a lot actually, but she didn't want to get too serious with him. There were many better-looking boys on campus, and it was Lucas that she really liked.

I put down the notebook. Possessive, jealous—surely it must be the same Grant? So, she had known him long before she met Lance.

The diary entries fizzled out. The rest of the notebook was blank apart from a few attempts at poetry in the back pages. I wondered if the second book would shed more light on what had happened to her.

I looked at my watch—almost time for lunch. I picked up the second diary, a thick red hardback. Quickly flicking through the pages, I saw that this one was completely filled with writing.

The one good thing about not working for an employer was that my time was my own. I could spend the day as I wished, wasting my time doing absolutely nothing but the necessary chores around the house like tidying up the living room and bedroom, and washing up and cleaning the kitchen surfaces, before going off to meet up with old friends, drink coffee and chat. Or if I felt in an industrious mood, I could do a complete spring clean while my blokes were out of the house. Sometimes I even—after a couple of cups of coffee and perhaps a chocolate or two, three, or four—got down to the business of writing. The only downside was that I didn't have a regular income of my own. Of course, we weren't destitute. Gerry was doing quite well, moneywise, and always seemed to be busy, and Daniel was paying me more than enough for his bed and board. But the little I had already earned from my published short stories was such a bonus. The first cheque I spent on a glamorous evening dress I would have very little chance to wear. Apart from one or two Christmas 'dos' and special birthdays, there were very few occasions that required me to 'dress up'. The next couple of payments went straight into my bank account, where they were swallowed up with Gerry's earnings and used to pay for the regular bills that came in.

I looked forward, therefore, to a whole afternoon binge-reading Hazel's life. Dan would be home between half past three and four, and Gerry knocked off about five, so I would have an uninterrupted session. I hoped that all my questions would soon be answered.

I sat in the easy chair, then got up and pulled it

towards the front window to bask in the afternoon sunlight. Outside it was chilly, but indoors, sitting in the pool of sunlight, it was warm. I opened the thick, red-covered notepad.

The words were written in an adult hand, more fluid, the letters less defined; an adult hand that smacked of an educated, calm, positive mind. There were no crossings-out, nothing added to the main body of the writing. Perhaps she had written it out roughly first, or maybe she just had a more organised mind than mine. I briefly mused what a shame it was that that mind had become fractured and confused as Hazel descended into dementia.

I read on.

MARCH 1965

My name is Hannah Elizabeth Hezekiah. I am known by the name of Hazel and I have reverted to the surname of Taylor, that of my first husband, Lance Taylor. I am twenty-four years old and have been accused of murdering my second husband, Grant Chase. My lawyer insists that I will be acquitted. He is not even convinced that I will be convicted of manslaughter. He is sure the jury will clear me and Grant's death will be recorded as accidental.

So Hazel began writing this in custody. Her lawyer was wrong about her being cleared of all charges. She had, initially, been convicted of manslaughter, but this was quickly overturned and her conviction quashed on appeal.

She continued: *I am writing this to set the*

record straight. I want to put things right. I am dedicating this diary to you, Marion, because I think—I hope—that you will understand why I did what I did and forgive me. By the time you read this I shall be dead. Lance has gone, Grant has gone, and I hope that everything will be forgotten and pass away as we three have. But before I leave this world, there are things I need to get off my chest. Perhaps I need to make my peace with the Almighty. I am hoping that he, like you, will forgive my weaknesses.

She began to explain that, at the time of Grant's death, she had been under great stress. Pregnant with Lance's child, her marriage to Grant had been disintegrating. She told of the quarrels they had and her fear that he would beat her and damage the unborn child. She wanted to leave him but didn't know where to go. She worried that wherever she went, Grant would find her and punish her.

She had become confused, and she worried about her mental state. She knew her mother had gone mad and was institutionalised when she grew older.

The day of the incident, she decided to run away to Cardiff, where she had lived before with Lance. She wasn't sure how to get there, but she knew she had to catch a train.

All this I knew before, apart from the fact that her mother had been sectioned. Hazel's words confirmed Sarah's suspicions.

I should never have married Grant, she wrote.

But I felt I owed it to him because of what had gone before. I was lost after Lance's death and Grant stepped in. I thought that it was fate. That I should have married him before and not Lance. But now I know I was wrong.

What had gone before? I was intrigued. Her words seemed to prove what I had already guessed— she had met Grant when she was a student at Leeds University.

CHAPTER TWENTY-ONE

The notepad was heavy, and my arms ached. I sat at the dining table and moved a vase of flowers to clear a space for it.

A new entry, again addressed to my mother, read:

I have done bad things in my life, but you have been a loyal friend, Marion, and I always felt I could come to you for comfort and advice. When I lost Lance, you were there for me. I want to tell you things now I have never told anyone else.

I used to keep a diary when I was younger, and I still have it to remind me of who I really am and what has happened to me in the past. I have always managed to conceal it amongst my clothes, first with Lance and then with Grant. Lance would not have held my past against me, because he was an open-minded man, but for some reason I kept it secret. I had to hide it from Grant because he was a jealous person and thought he owned me. He would have used the knowledge of my early pregnancy as yet another excuse to control me.

If I am sent to prison, I want you to keep that diary safe and to take it and this home with you, away from prying eyes.

I was not aware that Hazel had given anything

to my mother. Perhaps because she was released so soon "without a stain on her character", as the appeal judges worded it, Hazel had managed to retain her personal possessions.

I read further.

At university I was happy until I became tied up with Grant Chase. It happened like this…

Hazel liked a boy called Lucas, and although he was one of her main circle of friends, he was more attached to a girl called Jenny. Hazel did her best to catch his eye. When he remarked that he liked a red dress that she wore, she took to wearing it more often. She had her hair permed in the latest 'bubble-cut' style. She began to wear make-up regularly. But although he was always friendly to her, it was always Jenny that Lucas sat by, Jenny that he shared his sandwiches with, Jenny's arm he took when they were walking together in a gang.

It was Grant that was always staring at Hazel. She found it disconcerting at times because he wasn't really her type at all. She liked tall, fair men—a fact she found strange, given that she was small and dark and of Jewish descent. Grant, too, was dark-haired, slim and of average height. He once tried to kiss her at a party, but she kept him at arm's length, made the excuse she needed the bathroom, and got quickly away from his advances. He was cross with her.

When she finally cottoned on to the fact that Lucas and Jenny were in love and that Lucas had eyes only for his sweetheart, she succumbed to

Grant's repeated requests for a date.

I did like him—but not in a romantic way. I had a sort of rage inside me. I think I wanted to make Lucas jealous. Stupid really. He wasn't interested in me, only as a friend.

Hazel and Grant went to the cinema, but she didn't see much of the film.

Grant was all over me. Tangled up in his arms, I was hot and uncomfortable and annoyed with myself for becoming aroused.

She could not shake off his attentions. He came round to her college room every day, and she found it harder and harder to resist his advances.

There was a party in the students' lower common room. I can't remember what occasion it was. Maybe it was the end of term before Christmas, maybe someone's birthday. There were lots of balloons, many of them orange, there was loud music—rock and roll mainly—and lots of bodies dancing and jiving. I wore a flared blue flowery dress with lots of petticoats beneath it and my best white peep-toed sandals. I remember singing along to Buddy Holly.

Someone turned the lights out. I lost my friends. I needed to find the ladies' room because I had had too much to drink. I stumbled as I pushed open the glass doors and went into the corridor. I shared a cigarette with a girl in the toilets and then I left to go back to the party.

"Hazel," someone whispered and caught me around the waist. I recognised Grant's voice and the smell of his talcum powder. He pulled me

along the corridor and outside through the double doors. I was in no fit state to defend myself. He pressed me up against the wall and kissed me. I responded. Then he pulled up my dress. I was too tipsy to know what was happening at first, but when I realised he had entered me, I tried to pull away but he was too strong for me. When it was over, I cried, but he said. "Don't tell me you didn't enjoy it. You're not a virgin."

Oh Marion, Marion, it was true. You will have read in my other journal of how I was raped by my foster father and gave birth to his child when I was only fourteen. I had tried to forget it, but it was only four years previously and the memory kept resurfacing.

When I came out of the home for unmarried mothers, Lucy and Tom Smith would not have me back. I was glad because I never wanted to see that man again. I was sent to a children's home and was there for two years, one of eight children looked after by a couple who lived-in and a series of carers or "Aunties". I had been appointed a social worker, and when I was sixteen, I was transferred to a hostel with a warden in charge. I stayed there, going to a local grammar school, sitting my O- and A-levels, doing well enough to gain entry to university. I thought at last my life would change and I would get a new start in life. Grant Chase put paid to that.

He came to my room every night after that party and expected to have sex with me. I tried to fend him off with every excuse I could think of, but often he would not take no for an answer. I began to dread each evening and the knock on my door. If I pretended to be out or asleep, he would knock even louder, and I was afraid of him waking up my adjoining housemates. So I let him in. I was beginning to hate him.

When I discovered I was pregnant, I wanted to end it all. I confided in my friend Jean. She bought me a bottle of gin and advised me to have hot baths. My skin was red, but the baby refused to go away. I did not know how to kill myself. I went every day to the nurse for aspirins and was stockpiling them until one day the nurse stopped me.

I knocked at her door.

She ushered me in and said curtly, "Sit down!"

Then she asked me if there was anything wrong. I could not answer her.

She waited and then said, "If you won't tell me, I shall have to guess. Are you in the family way?"

I would not cry. I would not. She must have registered my distress from the look on my face. She touched my arm.

"Don't throw it all away," she said. "You've come so far."

She had no idea how far. I was so afraid I might cry.

"I would advise you to get rid of it," she said gently, "but it's not legal, although in some cases it might be the right thing to do. But there are options." She advised me to see the dean.

I could not tell Grant for a while. I knew what

his reaction would be. He had a temper, which I had borne the brunt of if he thought I was giving too much attention to another boy. He did not like that I still had my old coterie of friends. He had never been one of the 'inner' set, just on the periphery with mutual acquaintances. He was reading English literature as I was, so I could not escape him even at lectures. We continued to have sex until one day I plucked up courage to tell him my news.

"Your stupid girl!" he exclaimed.

"How is it my fault?"

"Girls know things. And they know how to get rid of babies. Get rid of it."

"Why couldn't you have used those French letter things?"

And then he hit me.

My friend Jean found me crying in the lavatories. She thought I had miscarried the baby.

"No. I'm crying because I <u>can't</u> get rid of it. It won't go."

The dean was very distant. An intellectual, he seemed to have his head in the clouds. A pale, tall, thin man, he looked down his long nose at me.

"What do you propose to do?"

I didn't really know. I just had to get away from there and from Grant.

"I want a transfer to another university."

"Mm. It might not be possible. What are your intentions about the baby?"

"I don't know. I have no parents, no family. I

suppose I shall have to give it up for adoption."
Again.

"Ah yes." He had a file on his desk. Was it mine?

"I need to see my social worker."

He seemed surprised. "Do you still have one? Do you know his or her telephone number?"

"Certainly." I gave it to him.

* * *

I did not tell Grant about the transfer. He had not been to see me since I'd told him about the baby. The only people who knew about it were my closest friends—Jean, Sylvia and Jenny. And Jenny had not revealed it even to Lucas.

On the day I left Leeds, my social worker met me at college and we carried two large boxes to her car. They held all my earthly possessions. As the car drew out through the college gates, I saw Grant with some of his mates. Our eyes locked. He looked alarmed. But then we drove out, and he was gone from my life. Forever, I thought.

I was transferred to Cardiff University. Far enough away from Leeds and Grant. I stayed at yet another home for unmarried mothers. You could say I was becoming an old hand at this. Every day I would travel to college, attend lectures and tutorials, and then go back to the home and eat baked beans on toast or tinned soup. I was always hungry. The other girls were the same. We filled up on bread and numerous cups of tea. I had been a juvenile at the other place and was much better cared for. Here, again, I was one of the youngest; the others were in their early twenties. But we were more or less left to our own devices. There was a matron-in-charge who gave us an allowance, but we had to make our own food and help with the laundry and cleaning. I chose to do the laundry as I loved to see and smell fresh sheets and clothes hanging outside on the washing line. I missed Jean and Jenny and Sylvia, the camaraderie of the other students and my old college. I did not want to get too close to my new pregnant friends, for we would part and never see each other again when our babies were born.

As my pregnancy progressed, I became very tired and unable to concentrate on my studies. Reluctantly I went to see the dean, this time a rather stout old boy with a pink face and a genial manner. He quite understood why I wished to leave and he hoped I would pick up my studies later on as I was quite an able student. I almost wept in front of him. Once again, I felt that life had pulled the rug from underneath me.

From then on, my whole life revolved around the home, visits from my new social worker, my daily chores and the lives of the girls around me. Some of them were very earthy. One Irish lass made me laugh. She swore a lot; nearly every word was an expletive, but somehow it didn't sound coarse coming from her. And despite her predicament, very similar to mine, she always *found something to laugh about and made the rest of us see the funny side of things. And when she was pleased, everything was "grand".*

CHAPTER TWENTY-TWO

I met Lance Taylor not long before my baby was born. I literally bumped into him on Queen Mary Street. Knocked into a wall. I banged my head. He went to apologise automatically, then when he saw my condition his apologies became more profuse.

I thought I would stop breathing when I saw him. He was the very image of the perfect man that I carried around in my head. Tall, broad-shouldered, blond-haired, handsome. He thought I was going to faint. I'm afraid that it was pure lust.

He had lost his pals, who had run on. Perhaps they were racing to a rugby match. He did not seem to mind that they had disappeared into the crowd.

He caught my arm. "Look here, are you all right?"

I held my hand to my head. No blood. But I did feel dizzy. Really.

"I think you need to sit down and have a glass of water."

He steered me into a nearby café and spoke to the man behind the counter.

I sat at a table and he brought me a glass of water. He examined my head. "That's a nasty bump; you'll probably get a bruise. I'm so sorry.

I don't usually go bashing young women about."

The waiter brought a cup of coffee. I sipped my water.

"Oh, I'm sorry. Would you like one?" He indicated his cup.

I nodded. I wanted this moment to last as long as possible. While we waited for my coffee, we introduced ourselves. He shook my hand.

"So what are you doing here in Cardiff, Hazel?" he asked. "You don't sound Welsh and you haven't got a Cardiff accent."

"I'm at the university," I lied.

"Oh, a brainy girl," he laughed.

"What about you?"

"I'm a plumber."

"Do you like it?"

"It's okay."

While we drank our coffee, we continued to talk and find out about each other. I was already smitten by this hunk with blond hair and blue eyes.

"You will miss the match," I said.

"Oh, that's all right." He seemed very relaxed about it. "When is the baby due?"

"In a month."

"Looking forward to it?"

My face froze. "No."

He seemed very surprised. "Every baby is a joy. A gift."

"Not if you have to give birth."

He smiled. "Yeah. Well, I'm a man. I don't have to go through all that."

"It was a mistake. A terrible mistake."

He stopped smiling. "Oh, I'm sorry. I didn't mean to…"

I suddenly wanted to leave and stood up, but my legs seemed to buckle under me and I had to sit down.

"You're not about to drop it here, are you?"

Despite his attempt at humour, I could see he was concerned. He told me he had a car parked nearby and that he would take me home.

"Wait here," he commanded.

When he had gone, I smiled to myself. I had found a Sir Galahad.

She was a very lucky lady. And then I pondered. Were you laying it on a bit thick, young Hazel? You saw he felt guilty, and you used it. Still, I didn't blame her.

I gathered up my shabby plastic handbag and my bag of shopping and leaned on his arm as he led me outside to the car, breathing in the smell of his woolly duffle coat. He waxed lyrical about his car. It was just a car to me. I only knew them by colours, not makes.

When we stopped at the tall building on the outskirts of the city, he asked, "Are you sure this is where you live?"

I nodded. The houses must have been owned by well-to-do folk at one time. They had bay windows downstairs; some had three storeys. Most had been converted into offices, dental surgeries and flats. There was no sign outside the home to advertise to outsiders what it was. A plaque simply said St. Barnaby's. I thought it amusing that I, born a Jew, should be a resident of a Catholic home for unmarried mothers. But I didn't really have a faith as such. I knew nothing about Judaism, having been parted from my mother at such a young age. I had been sent to Sunday School as a child and sang about "Gentle Jesus, meek and mild", but I had never embraced Christianity. I suppose I was a heathen.

I hoped Lance thought the place was an apartment block or student accommodation.

"Do you need a hand? Are there stairs to climb?" He was very solicitous.

"No. I'm fine, really. I think I just had a dizzy turn."

"Well, I think you should see a doctor. Just to be on the safe side."

I did not know how to get him to stay, this gentle giant. I felt so safe with him. But I thanked him, left the car and went inside the home, my home.

The nurse examined me. She was not concerned about the bump to my head, but she said my blood pressure was high. I was taken to hospital. I heard the term "pre-eclampsia" for the first time and wondered what it meant. I became worse while I was in hospital and lost consciousness. I then hovered between sleep and wakefulness. I was aware of white coats; there was a painful tugging. I felt sick. Then I heard a baby cry.

When I awoke properly, I sensed a presence in the room. A nurse swished over to me.

"Ah, you're with us."

I blinked. The light seemed very bright.

The nurse pulled the blind down over the window. "Is that better?"

"Thank you."

"Do you want to see your baby?"

"Baby? No."

"She's beautiful." She lifted her out of the cot by my side. "Look, isn't she perfect?" She drew back the lacy shawl to reveal the infant's face.

She was indeed a lovely baby. Dark, dark hair, a perfectly formed little face, button nose. She opened her eyes and looked straight at me. She knew. She knew.

"What do you think you'll call her?"

"Rachel." It was the first name that came into my head. My mother's name.

She must have been new, this nurse. I knew I could not keep this baby.

* * *

I put a bookmark in the diary to mark the page and stretched. *Ow!* A touch of cramp in my leg. I hobbled downstairs, put some lamb chops in the oven and then peeled some potatoes for dinner. My mind was full of Hazel as I prepared the meal.

Gerry came home and pressed his freezing cold hands on my neck, making me jump.

"Don't do that!" I scolded.

After dinner, I revealed to him everything I had read.

"So that solves the mystery of Rachel, then," he said.

"Maybe. But what happened to Marianne? Come to that, where was Rachel when Hazel and Lance came to live in our street?"

Gerry helped me clear the table. "I'll wash up. I know you're dying to get back to Hazel's diary."

I kissed him and flew upstairs. I was still reading when Gerry came to bed later.

"Listen to this!" I told him.

He groaned.

* * *

Hazel went back to St. Barnaby's with the baby while arrangements for adoption were made. Some of the girls cried terribly when their babies were taken away. Hazel just felt a dullness inside. She could not keep this baby. It was Grant's and she did not want it. She refused to look at its face; it reminded her too much of Grant. Why didn't they take the baby away?

"The baby's crying."

It was the new nurse again who came bustling in. Didn't she understand? I didn't care. The nurse, Mary, came and sat on my bed and took my hands in hers.

"Whatever happened, it's not your baby's fault. She'll be gone soon and then you'll miss her, you know. It won't be easy. You're hardening your heart. I suppose that's understandable; you don't want to get too close to her. But Hazel, I want you to know we're here for you."

She looked at me sadly and then walked over

to the cradle. Without another word exchanged between us, she took the baby out of the bedroom to feed her.

And then one day, the baby—Rachel—had gone. I went over to her cot and it was empty. Someone must have taken her while I was in the bath. Not even a shawl or a bootee was left to show she had lain there.

I don't know what came over me. I suddenly felt bereft and ran downstairs to see the matron-in-charge.

"Someone's taken Rachel!"

"Yes. You knew it was coming, Hazel. You signed the consent form. Your social worker was here when you signed."

I broke down in tears. The bitch! The bitch! The matron came around the desk, gave me a handkerchief and patted me on my shoulder.

"She's gone to a very good home, dear. She'll have the best of everything."

Still the tears came. I had not cried for years. It was as if a dam had broken.

The matron waited. When I stopped crying, she said, "You can stay with us for a while, my dear. When you've got over the shock, you can be a comfort to the other girls. The social worker, Grace, is looking for a flat for you. You can resume your studies if you wish, have a new start. But you have a home here short-term. And you can give support to Jill and Bernadette when they have their babies adopted. You will understand how they feel."

She was not unkind. But no one knew how I felt.

Mary, the new nurse, came to see me. I was done crying and sat listlessly on my bed. I knew that Mary had wanted me to keep my baby.

"You will never forget her, you know, Hazel. You will always be looking for her and wondering where she is and what she looks like."

I looked away. I had got over the initial shock. Now, with my senses restored, I knew it was what I had wanted. But Mary wouldn't understand.

CHAPTER TWENTY-THREE

By this point, I had realised that Hazel was quite a storyteller and I was quite enthralled. I thought, too, how sad it was back then when it was a scandal to conceive a baby out of wedlock. How times have changed, that many women can decide to have children even without a husband, in this day and age.

I knew it was late, but I wanted to carry on reading.

And then one day I was shopping in Queen Street when I saw a face I knew in the crowd. That lovely big man. What was his name? Lance. Stepping on toes and elbowing my way, I propelled myself through the crowd until I was right next to him. Would he remember?

He saw me and stopped. "Hello."

People surged past us. He looked down. My bump had gone.

"So you had the baby. What was it?" He smiled.

"A girl. I named her Rachel, after my mother."

"How lovely."

He smiled and my heart soared. I wanted this man to love and protect me. How could I keep him? There were people all around us. Then I fainted.

When I came to, Lance was fanning me with

a newspaper. A woman was keeping people from treading on me. I was lucky—because of the crush of people, I had not gone slap bang down on the pavement. We were in the doorway of Woolworths. A man—I take it he was a security officer—asked Lance if I was all right. Lance was kneeling down in front of me. It was so embarrassing.

"I'm fine. I'm fine." I struggled to my feet, Lance assisting me.

"Do you want me to call an ambulance?" The security man asked.

"No, no, no!" I cried. "I'm fine. Really."

"You go on, Phil," Lance said to someone next to him—I presumed it was a mate. He looked at me severely. "Are you living in the same place? I think I ought to take you home!"

And that was how I met Lance Taylor. He was a kind, generous, easy-going fellow, and I played on his sympathetic nature.

When we stopped outside the large brick building, I told him I had a confession to make and that it was a place for unmarried mothers. He seemed not in the least fazed. Perhaps he had guessed. I told him that my mother had died and I had no other family and that the father of my baby had abandoned me. The only people I knew who cared about me were my social worker, Grace, and the staff at the home.

"So, what happened to the baby—Rachel?" he asked gently.

I told him I had given her up for adoption because I had no means of support.

He looked very sad. "You do know they'll probably change her name?"

I shrugged.

"But you may want to find her later and she'll be known by another name. You may have difficulty tracing her."

I would never want to find her. Without her, I was free. Free from the ties of early motherhood, free from the shackles of Grant. The only person I wanted right then was this wonderful man who sat beside me. To look into his face every day and to be cared for by him was my intention.

I told Lance that I could not stay at St. Barnaby's indefinitely; they needed my bed for other unfortunate girls. I had a social worker who was looking for a flat or a house that I could share with other young women. She had also lined up interviews for jobs for me. One was the very next day at a C & A clothes store. He was very concerned.

"I'm sure I'll land on my feet," I told him as I left the car.

The next day, Bernadette, a fortnight away from her due date, puffed up the stairs.

"Hazel, there's a young man downstairs in Madam's office asking for you. If he's the fecking father of your babe, why on earth are you here with us? It's with him you should be." She grinned, a wide, knowing smile. "Sure, and I can see why you fell for his child. He's just grand."

I ran down and collided with him in the downstairs corridor.

"Hey," he grabbed hold of my arm.

The matron-in-charge came out of the office. *"Hazel, I don't approve of you meeting young men here!"*

I beamed at her. *"He's not my young man. Are you?"* I turned to Lance. He shook his head imperceptibly. *"He brought me home when I fainted yesterday."*

Lance turned to the matron. *"I just wanted to make sure she's all right."* He smiled at me. *"Did you get the job?"*

"I did."

I smiled at matron. I could not stop smiling. *"Just popping out. Won't be long."*

Outside he said, *"I thought we could celebrate with a cup of coffee somewhere. Fancy the Kardomah?"*

His car was parked around the corner.

"How can you stand it in that place? It's so dingy."

"Well, where else could I go?" I spread my arms out. *"It's not bad. We get fed. And I'll be out of there soon."*

"Has your social worker found you a place yet?"

"I have to look at a flat tomorrow. I'll be sharing with a couple of other girls. I don't start work till next week, so Grace is going to pay my rent for me till I get paid."

"Don't forget you'll have to work a week in hand."

"Oh, yes." I'd forgotten about that.

Over coffee we found out more about each other. I told him I'd grown up in and around London. My mother had been seriously ill and had died so I was raised by foster parents. I'd been at Leeds University when I fell pregnant. "I transferred to Cardiff."

"Why?"

"I just felt everything in my life was going wrong and I wanted to get away. I could go back to college if I wanted to, you know. They still had a place for me. But I wrote and told the registrar I could not take it up."

"That's a shame. You should have."

"How would I survive?"

"You'd get a grant, surely?"

"But what about day to day expenses?"

"Wouldn't social services help you?"

"They're not going to keep me, Lance. I'm classed as an adult now."

"I see."

After coffee, we decided to go to the pictures and I was late getting back to St. Barnaby's. Matron had a face like thunder. She was just going off duty and Clarissa, one of the senior nurses, was taking over for the night shift.

"No good will come of this!"

"Of what?"

"Staying out late with a young man you hardly know. Mark my words, you'll be in the family way again soon, as sure as eggs is eggs."

"Mrs Goode. He's just a friend."

But I got to know him very well that autumn. It

was platonic at first. Being a genuinely kind person who was concerned about my predicament, he came to visit me at the home once more, and from then on we met in the city centre. A couple of times, he came to see me at C & A, and I was pleased to see him but told him he should wait for me outside—I didn't want to get into trouble and lose my job.

We were both pleased when I moved into the flat. It was pretty basic accommodation, but he bought me a few things to make it more homely: red cushions, an orange pouffe, a picture of a country scene I'd said I liked. My own wages were not enough to lash out on luxuries, but I did buy some nice clothes and a good pair of shoes. Lance became more romantic now that we could get together away from St. Barnaby's, but I kept him at arm's length and reminded him that I did not want to end up in the home again.

"The Home for Fallen Women," he laughed. "Quite apt in your case, since you seem to have a penchant for falling at my feet."

He was such an easy-going chap to be with and completely non-judgemental. I was so relaxed in his company. Bernadette came to visit me with her tiny baby. Her family had forgiven her for her lapse, so she had decided to keep the baby and return home. I presumed she meant Ireland, but there were lots of Irish people in Cardiff. I cooed over the baby, a girl she had called Theresa, but was so glad I no longer had a child. Theresa slept most of the time, but when she woke up, her crying got on my nerves. Bernadette brought me a lavender and cream bedspread that she had spent hours crocheting. As I wrote my diary in the evenings, she sat and crocheted.

I could not find the diary when I moved. Bernadette told me that Clarissa had found it under my bed and taken it to Mrs Goode. Thank goodness I still had my old one, with my secrets and my mother's letters tucked inside. Although I never looked at any of those letters anymore—it was too painful—I concealed all my personal stuff with my underwear. It was my only link with my past.

I went to St. Barnaby's.

"I believe you have something of mine in your possession," I told the matron.

She knew what I meant. She did not deny it. "I've destroyed it."

"That's theft. It was my property. You had no right to take it or destroy it!"

I knew why she'd burnt it. After Lance's visits, I had come to view the place with different eyes. I was ashamed of it. It was run-down and grubby. There were repairs that needed doing, the walls in the kitchen were damp, the whole place needed redecorating and refurbishing.

All these thoughts I had consigned to paper. I forgot the kindness of the staff, I forgot how tight the finances were. All my comments had been so negative. I was ashamed; I could see why Mrs Goode was angry with me. Strange really, when you consider my background. I had nothing to be *uppity about. But Lance had put ideas into my head about what to expect from life. He did not want to settle for second best of anything.*

"Mrs Goode, I'm sorry. I'm just a pretty selfish girl, I think."

She softened. "Hazel, grasp the opportunities in life that God gives you from now on, with both hands. May God go with you."

And I left almost blinded by tears.

CHAPTER TWENTY-FOUR

Hazel continued with what Lance had told her about his background.

"My family were quite well off. My dad's an accountant and my mother is a lawyer. I was never the most intelligent one of my siblings. My two younger sisters were the brainy ones; they went to university. Alice is a journalist in Sydney and Kate is in publishing. As the only boy, I was spoilt rotten, but it soon became obvious that higher education was not for me. I was good with my hands and I loved cars and machines. I tried a couple of jobs in factories and that, but then I became an apprentice plumber.

"By then my parents had decided to go back to Australia. Dad's folks are Australian, and he had come over in his early twenties for a holiday, met my mother, got a good job and stayed. So off they went, and I was left behind. The girls were still in high school then."

"Have you ever been to visit them?" I asked.

"Twice. Mum and Dad paid my fare. And they've been over twice."

"But you came back."

"God, it was hot. A bit too hot. Lovely house, big garden, swimming pool—very nice. Great outdoor life. But I was quite happy to return. I'd met a girl and fallen in love. She was the girl of my dreams."

"What happened to her?"

He frowned. "She went off with someone else and I was heartbroken. At first, I was all over the place. But you get over these things." He squeezed my waist and smiled. "And then I met you. Everything's good now. I'm a qualified plumber with all my City and Guilds qualifications. I work for a good company and I'm earning good money. I've got my job, got my girl, got my car, and I'm renting a three-bedroom house with my good mate Phil."

"I've never been to your house. Where do you live?"

"In Whitchurch, a suburb just north of Cardiff."

"What were you doing in town when I first met you?"

"When I pushed a highly pregnant lady into a wall and nearly knocked her out?" He teased me. "I was going to a rugby match."

"I guessed as much. You never did see that match."

"No. But I know the score. Wales won." His eyes twinkled.

"And the second time?"

"The time you were so overcome by my handsome face that you fainted?"

How close to the truth he was.

"I have trouble with my blood pressure," I defended myself.

"Oh, oh," he laughed at me. "That's your

excuse, is it? If you want to know, I was shopping for a wedding present."

"Who for?"

"Shouldn't that be 'for whom', Miss Clever-Clogs?"

I punched him playfully on the arm, and he feigned injury.

"For Phil, as it happens. He's getting married in a couple of months' time."

"Did you get the present?"

"No. I got waylaid by a fallen woman. Actually, you could help me. I was thinking of buying a tea set or a blanket or something. Could we go shopping soon? You can help me choose something."

He was very quiet after I agreed to go shopping with him. Suddenly, he said. "When Phil gets married, I shall be on my own in that family-sized house. I'll need someone else to share with me. I don't want to be on my own."

I didn't catch on at first. At last, the penny dropped. "Are you asking me to move in with you? I've only just moved here."

"Don't you want to shack up with me? Am I that bad?" He pretended to be offended.

"It's not that. I… It's too soon."

"We're good together. We know everything about each other, don't we?"

I nodded dumbly.

"Actually, I was thinking of the two of us getting hitched."

"No."

"Why not?"

He told me he loved me. That when he first met me, he thought I was very sweet and pretty. Then when he took me home the second time, I had seemed so frail and vulnerable. It seemed so unfair that I should be regarded as a shameful person and put into that awful place.

"It wasn't that bad."

"Anyway, I felt so sorry for you and I wanted to help you out, and before I knew it, Hazel, I had fallen for you—hook, line and sinker."

He won me over, Marion. Completely. Looking back, it all seems too casual a decision to make, too spur of the moment, but I promise you it seemed so right at the time. Don't forget I had nobody else in the world except Grace, my social worker. My mother may have still been alive; I didn't know. But she was gone from my life and I was all alone.

I trusted Lance. For all his genial, happy-go-lucky nature, I felt I could rely on him. He would not let me down. So I said 'yes'.

Grace was not happy about the arrangement, but I was twenty years old and not a child. She met Lance and he won her over too. He seemed so genuine.

"I know things have been difficult for Hazel," he told her, *"but I'm doing well, and I want to look after her."* He winked. *"She needs someone to look after her. Every time she sees me, she falls down in a doorway."*

***

Lance had so many friends. There were people at our wedding I had never seen before. His parents, sisters and their boyfriends all came over from Australia and stayed in the Park Hotel. I wrote to my old friends from Leeds University, and Sylvia, Jean and Jenny came, Jenny now engaged to Lucas and proudly sporting her engagement ring and fiancé on her arm. Jean was my flower girl and carried a bouquet almost as big as mine. Bernadette, the Irish girl, was also invited to be a bridesmaid and brought her baby, but the infant bawled loudly during the service and had to be taken out. I had very few guests on my side of the church, but I didn't care. I was blissfully happy.

Lance had given me money to buy a wedding dress, and I went to David Morgan's to try on various lacy, floaty, frothy creations. I was going to be married in white, no matter what people might think. I felt like a princess. Jean and Bernadette had dresses very similar to mine but less decorated and ivory-coloured, not white.

Grace's husband, Wilf, was called upon to give me away. And despite her misgivings, Grace herself looked radiantly happy to see me so happy, getting joined to the man I loved. Neither of us had thought such a day would come so soon in my life.

It was one of my best days ever. There was only one time during the service when I suddenly felt sad. I missed my mother. Was she still alive? Where was she? She would have wanted to have been at my wedding. Then Lance smiled at me and winked, and my spirits were immediately lifted.

We didn't have a honeymoon. After our wedding at the small church in Whitchurch and a prolonged reception—called a wedding 'breakfast' in those days—which went on for a few hours, everyone eating and drinking, we went off in Lance's blue saloon car to our house not far away. Philip, Lance's friend, had been married a month before us and now lived in Swansea. He and his wife had been guests at our wedding and looked the perfect picture of a young married couple.

The house was now all our own. We didn't own it, of course. It was a rented property, but to me it was my first 'real' home. It was a modern semi-detached house with a white pebble-dashed surface. The actual owner had bought it, then had the chance of working abroad for a few years, so was renting it out until his return. Lance worked out that by then we would have saved enough money to buy a property of our own

Lance swept me up and carried me over the threshold. When he put me down, he kissed me and said, "Well, here we are then, Mrs Hazel Taylor. An honest woman at last."

I heard a faint snoring. Gerry had fallen asleep. I pushed the diary under the bed and switched off my bedside light. I'd left Hazel happy, and so I fell asleep quite soon, relaxed and peaceful.

CHAPTER TWENTY-FIVE

Hazel and Lance did not sleep together before the wedding. What started as a chance meeting grew into a friendship, and then events took on such an impetus that Hazel was married before she'd really thought of the consequences. She liked to tell people, "Lance rushed me off my feet—literally."

Hazel was afraid to have sex with Lance. She thought of the sweaty, grunting sessions with Grant and the outcome of those and was scared. The face of Tom Smith, for so long buried deep in the subconscious brain, now surfaced and made her feel sick, she told her diary.

"I don't want to get pregnant," I told Lance.

"That's all right, I'll use a French letter. Did you know that there are things women can have? You'll have to go and see a doctor. I've heard about this tablet that will soon be used by everyone—they call it 'the pill'."

Lance was tender, considerate and patient. He became alarmed one night early on in their marriage when Hazel woke up screaming.

"What is it? What is it?" He held me. "Did you have a bad dream? It's all right. It's over now. I'm here."

She clung to him, sobbing, and he soothed

her and stroked her. She knew she could not tell him everything that disturbed her mind. Out of the wad of bad experiences she'd suffered, she chose to tell him about her parents and the concentration camp. They lay awake together until dawn, and Lance listened as Hazel talked. He was seriously concerned. A happy-go-lucky person, he had grown up in a happy-go-lucky family that made the best of everything. He'd had a happy childhood, was indulged by his mother and had an easy relationship with his father. As an adult, he took things as they came. He could not begin to imagine what those awful days in Hazel's life must have been like. All he knew was that she was now his wife and he should do the best he could to relieve her of the burden of those terrible memories.

He knew he had to go to work, but he wanted to leave her in a better frame of mind.

"Do you remember anything about your first experience of this country? Did you go to school?"

"I was too young at first. Everything is a blur. I think we came over in a boat. I think I slept a lot. All I can remember is a feeling of rocking. I think I was sick—and hungry. Very hungry. Voices, faces, it's all a blur, Lance. I know I went to school in England; I can see a picture of desks in my mind sometimes—rows of wooden desks. And I remember singing. But it was all foreign to me at first. And gradually, the words came, but I can't remember much. Just snatches of things, you know. My first foster parents were kind, I think, but

I cannot remember much about them. There were so many strange faces. I was scared and clung to my mother, but then she left me. She was ill, and they took her to hospital."

So far so good. Everything Hazel wrote that she'd told Lance was true.

"What about your other foster parents?"

I could just imagine Hazel's face hardening.

"They were not nice to me."

"What did they do to you? Lock you in the coal shed?" Lance teased.

Oh, that wouldn't have gone down well.

"I'd prefer to forget that. But I had school and I learned English and I loved the poems and stories I read in class. I was quite happy in school."

I could imagine Lance looking at the clock.

"It's half past six. I start work at half seven. I've got to get up. You've had a rotten night; I suggest you have a lie-in."

"What about you? You'll be exhausted."

"Got to earn money. For us. Perhaps it's time you went back to work now."

"I've given in my notice at C & A."

"Why?"

"I want to learn typing and shorthand."

"Okay. Do it. There's courses—night school and that."

"Can we afford it?"

"Of course we can. As long as you remember I'm a hard-working man and I want my dinner on the table every day at six, wench." He slapped my bottom and left.

I could just imagine Hazel grinning at his departing back, stretching her limbs, warm in the knowledge that she had such a kind, caring husband. For the first time in her life, she felt safe. Really safe.

She wrote: *I knew I would be fine for the rest of the day. Daylight always dispelled my night terrors.*

Before Lance left the house, he brought me a cup of tea in bed and tickled my toes. I thought I was the luckiest woman in the world.

I called to Gerry as he left the bedroom. "You never tickle my toes!"

He came back in and gave me a puzzled look. "Tickle your toes?"

"Yes."

"You never tickle mine!"

I threw the pillow at him, but he ducked.

* * *

There was a gap in the diary, and the next entry was two years after Hazel's wedding. That meant she was about twenty-two years old. I could only imagine she'd been sublimely happy in the meantime, settling down to married life with Lance and enjoying her new status as a wife and a homemaker. Presumably, she completed the course on typing and shorthand and was too busy with that and housework and just living—as she had never lived before—in a secure relationship within her own home with a man who loved her.

If she'd had any bad dreams, presumably Lance comforted her, or maybe they had vanished since her marriage.

The reason for the new entry was that the man who owned their house was being transferred back to Britain and had sent them a letter via his letting agent to prepare them for the fact that they would have to move out sooner than he had anticipated. They would not need to go until their leasing contract was up, but Lance had to look around for another property to rent as he had not saved enough money to buy one in the immediate vicinity. He had been toying with the idea of starting his own business, but that would have to be put on hold for the foreseeable future.

After a few weeks, he became disheartened to find there were no houses for renting in the area, and as buying one was completely beyond his pocket, he decided to widen his search.

One day, Hazel wrote, *he came home very excited. He had found a property that was affordable, and if I got a job, we could manage the mortgage easily. Perhaps in a few years, the house would be paid for and he could think of starting up on his own. I asked him where the property was situated.*

"In the Valleys," he replied. "The houses are cheaper than here in Cardiff."

"Is it far away?"

I had never been to the Valleys before. I thought it was one place, not a series of individual places where each small community had its own colliery and existed independently.

Lance told me he could travel to work easily by car and, as he had to travel all over the county anyway, it would not make much difference to him.

"I might even buy myself a bigger car." He beamed and, hugging me, said, "It will be our very own home this time. Not rented. We will own it. And no one can turf us out."

I was pleased because he was pleased.

When I actually paid my first visit to Cwm Terrace in Aberbach, I had quite a shock. It was very different from the new semi-detached houses in the leafy street where we had been staying. My first impression was of rows and rows of drab terraces with grey slate roofed houses, some opening out directly on to the streets. There were women on the doorsteps staring at Lance's great big shiny car. To be honest, I was scared. What had we come to?

Lance must have seen the look of shock on my face. "It's okay, Hazel. The natives are friendly. I've already had a chat with some of them. The house itself is quite roomy and there's a nice long garden at the back." He squeezed my arm. "We'll be fine."

I never thought I would, but I got to love my new home, even though some of the streets were steep and, with a working coal mine, everything seemed coated in coal dust. I was very shy at first but got a job in a local bakery, and though some of the girls were a bit loud, they were good-natured. One of them—I think her name was Pat—had *kittens she wanted to find homes for. I took a little black one home and we called it Freddy. It amused us both with its antics. And it was at Aberbach I grew to understand how important it was to have good neighbours, because it was there that I met you and Reg, Marion.*

CHAPTER TWENTY-SIX

Siân, it was, who spoke to me first. I was hanging out the washing in the back garden when I became aware of someone watching me. She was evidently standing on a brick and peering over the stone wall. I could just see a pair of big brown eyes and a fringe of light brown hair.

"Hello," I said and smiled.

The head disappeared for a moment and then came back up, her curiosity getting the better of her guilt at being nosy.

I laughed aloud at this picture of myself.

"Hello," the girl replied. "I'm Siân. What's your name?"

"Hazel."

"That's a nut."

"Yes," I laughed.

"Can I come around and see your cat? Mam and Dad won't let me have a pet."

"Oh, that's sad. Yes, you may come around and see my cat. His name is Freddy."

"I heard him fighting last night. He woke me up. Dad said he'd throw a bucket of water over him next time."

"He did make a noise, didn't he? I think he's on another cat's territory."

"But I like cats."

"So do I."

And that is how I met you, Marion. Siân came to my house to see Freddy and then <u>we</u> got to talking in the street.

At this point, Marion, I have to be absolutely honest with you. My nightmares were much fewer at that time and I was very happy. You and Reg were good friends and kind people.

Lance was always busy. He put in a bathroom, converting the old washhouse and pantry. He smashed down the internal wall to turn the two rooms downstairs into one large living space. He relished living in such a close community. If anyone needed a job doing, he would be there helping. I realised I was seeing less and less of my husband. I still had my part-time job in the bakery, but I was spending more and more time in your house.

And then I received two shocks in a very short time. Completely out of the blue. The first was when my old pal Jean wrote to me. She had told me at my wedding that Grant Chase had been really upset when I left Leeds suddenly without telling him. He had stayed at uni and got a mediocre degree. After everyone had left and gone their separate ways, Grant became just a name from the past. Jean had stayed in Leeds and married Johnny, who was from that area.

Johnny had recently seen Grant in the park. They were surprised to find out they had both stayed in the city. Johnny told him he had married Jean and they were expecting their first child.

Grant was still single. He was excited because he'd gone into business management and was moving to Cardiff to take over as manager of a large store. Nobody had told Grant where I had moved to when I left uni. Jean thought she had better let me know he was coming my way.

Well, Marion, I was shocked to the core. My nightmares returned. I did not want to see that man again. I had no one to turn to but you. I could not tell you about the baby I had given up. I told you about the concentration camp to elicit your sympathy. I have never revealed the truth about Rachel to you before. I thought you might hate me.

No, my mother would not have hated anyone who had found themselves in the situation Hazel had been in. But Hazel would not have known that at this stage.

The second shock was when Lance broke down in tears and confessed that he had been unfaithful.

My anchor in life, Hazel wrote. *My big, beautiful husband reduced to this. He told me that I had not been responsive to him for some time. He had been attracted to a girl who worked at a pub. They had flirted and she was, in his words, 'up for a bit'. I was shocked, Marion, but I forgave him completely. How was Lance to know that the reason I had shunned him was because visions of Grant loomed up in my memory and any act of physical intimacy at that time was out of the question?*

Lance left me. Alone, I really suffered. I began doing strange things. I would walk into a room and forget why I had gone in there. I would stare into space and then realise it was dark outside and I had not drawn the curtains or switched on the light. I don't know if the neighbours noticed, but you and Reg never changed your attitude to me. You took me as I was and always gave me a sympathetic ear.

And then Lance returned to me. He knocked on the door knocker! It was his own house. When I opened the door, he stood there looking sheepish.

"Am I forgiven?"

"Oh Lance, Lance!" I threw myself into his arms. He would never know how much I needed him then.

After this he told me he thought we should start a family.

"I know you had a bad time. You got caught out. It happens. It is a shame you had to have her adopted; I know how you must have felt. It's a pity but you must put that behind you now. You mustn't be afraid. I will not leave you again, I promise."

My eyes brimmed with tears. I know I had been somewhat economical with the truth, as they say, and not told him everything about my past. And yes, I was afraid. I knew that someone like Lance would expect a large family. Surrounded by children, he would be a happy man. Somehow, I had to put the past to bed.

And now I will break off because I fear my

waters have broken. I shall have to ring the bell to let the nurses know.

I realised with a start that everything I had read up to this point had been written when Hazel was in custody, waiting for her trial. This must have been a false alarm because, looking at the date, her trial was the week after, and Hazel had still been pregnant then. The birth must have taken place not long after she was sentenced. There had been a huge public outcry at the decision, and petitions raised. The Home Office had stepped in, and Hazel's appeal had been launched almost immediately afterwards.

I still had a few questions in my mind that needed answering. When had she met up with Grant, and what had happened to the baby, Marianne?

But I had read myself into a stew. The housework was being neglected. I had not made any more adjustments or amendments to my manuscript. Gerry was not a complaining man, but even he had noticed that the house was not as tidy as it usually was.

Daniel was blunter in his criticism. He ran his finger over the mantelpiece.

"This house could do with some dusting," he commented.

"Why don't you get a duster and do it then?" I snapped.

"Ooh! Isn't that your job?"

"If you don't like it here, move out and find your own place!"

"Maybe I will," he rejoined.

What was happening to me? To us? Hazel was taking over my life.

Rachel rang me. "Well, have you opened the parcel?" She was on my back straight away.

I hedged. "There are photographs; I have no idea who they are. Maybe some of you as a baby. And some letters. From her mother."

"Is that all? Why would she want to leave them to you? Why not to me? After all, Rachel was my grandmother!"

"I know. When I have read through them, you shall have them."

She backed off slightly. "Well get on and read them then!"

"I shall."

I turned my attention to my home and family. I cleaned through the house, washed and ironed a pile of laundry, and even had a tussle with my script. My menfolk said nothing, but there seemed less tension in the air.

I did not resume reading Hazel's diary until over a week later. I found the place where the narrative had broken off and settled myself in an armchair, feet underneath me, a cup of coffee and two chocolate biscuits alongside me on a small nest of tables.

Hazel must have had her baby when she wrote this. Perhaps she'd been awaiting the outcome of her appeal. There was no date.

CHAPTER TWENTY-SEVEN

It was in the Hayes in Cardiff that I caught sight of Grant Chase. I had been to Howell's to buy a coat to wear at a neighbour's wedding. I'd splashed out more than I normally did for clothes, which I usually bought in the local shops, but I wanted something nice. My old brown woollen coat was becoming threadbare in places. Lance had bought me a fur coat, but I hardly ever wore it—it seemed out of place in Aberbach.

Then, as I paid for some oranges at a stall, I saw him. Just before he saw me. In hindsight, I should have turned my back, run away, but I stood frozen to the spot. While in this state, he rushed over to me. I was so shocked I dropped my string bag and Lance's oranges rolled all over the ground. Grant ignored them.

"Hazel! Hazel! Fancy meeting you here! I didn't know you lived in Cardiff."

He had filled out a bit, no longer a thin, wiry teenager. His hair was a little longer, his face still long and lean. It was definitely him. I recovered from my shock and stooped down to retrieve my damaged fruit.

"Let's go for a coffee," he suggested and propelled me by the elbow to the café on the Hayes, where he ordered coffee for me and a

black tea for himself. He did not ask about the baby. He must have presumed I'd had an abortion.

"How is life treating you?" he asked.

"Very well. I'm married."

I had to tell him. He must not think he could get back into my life, or back into my drawers for that matter.

"Where are you living?"

I must not tell him. I did not want him coming around to my house. Something told me he would. Strangely enough, once we began talking I lost all fear of him. He could not touch me now. I had Lance. Lance was my saviour.

"The Valleys," I replied, sipping my coffee, and quickly changed the subject. "How did you come to be in this neck of the woods?"

He was pleased to talk about himself. He told me he'd gone into retail management and how he'd been promoted to manager of a brand-new clothing store in Cardiff. Having no family and therefore no responsibilities, he'd jumped at the chance of more money. And so here he was, doing well for himself.

"What does your husband do?"

"Lance is a plumber."

"I see."

But he didn't see. The job didn't sound grand, but Lance was earning good money and he was seriously considering setting up his own business in a year or two.

"And what about you?"

"I work part-time in a bakery."

"Any children?"

I coloured. "No. Not yet."

"A waste of a good brain," he said.

"Pardon?"

"You're far too bright to be working part-time in a bakery."

"I used to work in C & A before I was married. And I've done a typing and shorthand course." I felt I had to defend myself.

He was thoughtful. "You could come and work for me. In the office, I mean. I need more staff. Reliable girls. It's good money—you could go far. What do you think?"

Marion, Marion, I was tempted. Grant could not hurt me again. I was well over him. I was a married woman. He must be over me by now. He could not touch me. I had Lance to protect me.

When I got home, I told Lance, "I've been offered a job with a new store in Cardiff. In the office. There's vacancies for clerks and typists. An old friend I used to know has just taken over as manager, and he thinks I'll be ideal."

I was quite excited.

"I thought we were trying for a family?"

Lance had stopped using contraception. I went behind his back and tried to get that new pill, but it was still being trialled and not on general prescription. My visit to the local GP had been a disaster. I could get pregnant any day.

"I suppose," Lance mused, "you could work there until you get pregnant. Or even for a bit longer. It would help us to save up for the baby

when it comes. Cots, baby clothes, pram—it all comes quite expensive."

"And nappies and bottles and baby baths and stuff," I added.

"Yes," he smiled. "Perhaps it would be good for you, too, to get out of the house and to use that brain of yours again." He tickled Freddy under the chin. "And this young scamp won't know what's hit him when the new baby arrives."

And so, Marion, that is how Grant Chase and I met for the second time. At first he left me alone—I saw him in the canteen a few times—but then he started coming to the office just when I was leaving. He walked me to the train station, Cardiff General (It's called Central now), and that was when things changed. The other girls in the office had gone home, but I had been given some last-minute work and was just covering my typewriter when Grant caught me alone.

"Hazel, Hazel."

"Hello, Grant. How are things?"

"Fine." He sat down on one of the other typists' chairs and put his feet up on the desk, to one side of the typewriter.

"I've never been able to get you out of my head, you know, Hazel."

"I expect you've had lots of girls since me."

"But I never forgot you, Hazel. You were the love of my life."

He rose from the chair and came over to the filing cabinet where I stood waiting to go home.

He turned me round, and with his index finger, tilted up my chin.

"Your sweet little face. That little nose. Those deep, dark eyes…"

"Grant! I'm a married woman."

He turned away. "I know. And I have to accept that. But we could get together now and then, couldn't we? Nothing serious. I'll get a room and you can join me after work. Your husband will never know. Just tell—Lance, is it?—that you've had to work late."

"No, no, no." I shook my head. "It's not going to happen, Grant. Lance is a good man—I would never do anything like that to him!"

"That's disappointing, Hazel. Why do you think I gave you this job?" He took my coat from the hook on the door. "Oh well, it was worth a try. Come on, I'll walk you to the station."

Before he left me at Cardiff General, he murmured, "Think about my suggestion," and then he went to catch his bus.

And then, dear Marion, you know what happened next. Lance died and I was in deep shock. While I was in mourning, Grant came around to the house in Cwm Street one night. Of course he had my records and had found out where I lived. I have to admit that I cried and he hugged me. Then he said that he should marry me.

"I've changed, Hazel. I know I hit you that time, and I've felt guilty ever since. I was young and stupid. I would never do such a thing again."

I told him I was pregnant and had been meaning to give my notice in.

"To lose your husband. With a baby on the way. That's going to be so hard for you. Let me take care of you and the baby."

I realised I should never have taken that job at the store. I had walked straight into Grant's trap.

On the other hand, I was completely alone in the world. I had no family. Grant was right; it was going to be very hard. He knew my early background, more or less, that I was a Jewish girl and a refugee. That I had been brought up in foster care. And that I had been pregnant at eighteen—by him. I knew he loved me, or was obsessed with me. So, though I knew that the neighbours thought my second marriage was indecently hasty so soon after Lance's death, I succumbed to Grant's continual coaxing, thinking it was the only way I could proceed. Maybe I wasn't in my right mind, I don't know.

The only thing we quarrelled about at that time was the fact I wanted to stay where I was in Aberbach, in Cwm Terrace. I felt safe there and I had my good neighbours, Marion and Reg. Grant wasn't greatly enamoured of the surroundings, but when I said I would only marry him if he agreed to live with me there, he gave in.

I had received so many flowers after Lance's death, the smell made me nauseous—due in part to my pregnancy, I suppose, but I could not bear the thought of having a big bouquet at my wedding.

My first wedding ceremony had been at a small

church in Cardiff with a crowd of Lance's friends and family, and I had worn a beautiful white dress. This time around, Grant and I were married in the local chapel, as you know, Marion. I chose an outfit resembling a wedding outfit as little as possible. I knew it was a garish colour, but I didn't care. You were so kind, altering the dress for me as I put on extra inches. And Siân was so sweet. I hadn't intended to carry anything, but she lent me her little handbag that almost matched my dress. At the last minute, a woman thrust a posy into my hand outside as I went in. You were so wonderful to me. And that woman, whoever she was.

I remembered it all clearly.

My marriage to Grant was a disaster from the start. I had been too hasty. I am always too hasty, Marion. Because I would not leave the house where Lance and I had been so happy, Grant had to sell the nice home he had in Llandaff. That really rankled with him. Then he was cross because I had photographs of Lance in the house. He took them down and threw them in the bin. I put all the rest of my photos and my secret things in an album and a folder and hid them in the attic when he was at work. I wrapped them up and put them behind the chimney.

As my pregnancy developed, I gave in my notice, and that was when things became really bad between Grant and me.

I put down the journal and unwrapped my cramped legs from underneath me. My coffee had grown cold on the table alongside me. I had been so engrossed in Hazel's story that I had forgotten about it.

I had only one more thing I needed to know: What became of the baby Marianne? Lance's baby. Or was it? Had Hazel caved in to Grant's demands?

I made myself another cup of coffee, and for lunch I had some cheese and crackers. Then I opened Hazel's journal. I skipped the next few pages about what happened at the station, and then I went back. I don't know why I did, but I found it quite disturbing.

I was so afraid. I never meant for him to fall in front of the train—just to go away. He said horrible things about me and then about Lance, and I put my hand up to his mouth to shut him up. He bit my hand to make me move it so he could carry on with his blasphemy, so I screamed and pushed him hard. I swear I did not mean to kill him.

When I realised what had happened, I wanted to run away. I felt faint. Then I saw my hand. His teeth marks were on my hand. So I worried them more and made my hand bleed. I was so scared.

Blimey! Did this mean that Hazel *was* guilty of manslaughter and had got away with it? And the bleeding hand—to make people sorry for her? But what if I had been Hazel—would I have done the same? Probably not. Hazel was a survivor. She had had to live on her wits.

Her report of the trial I skipped. And then there was nothing. Just a few lines. *I am free. My appeal has gone through. Thank the Lord.*

I sat and wondered what had been going on in Hazel's head. The fact she had written all this down for my mother—or me—to read seemed like a confession.

I turned over another page, and there was more writing. Would there be more revelations?

CHAPTER TWENTY-EIGHT

From the date, the next entry had been written quite a few years later. Where had Hazel been living then, and what had made her put pen to paper again?

My baby was born in hospital, and you and the prison staff were the only ones who came to visit me, so I named her Marianne in honour of you.

She was still addressing herself to my mother.

The baby was fostered while I remained in custody until the result of my appeal. When my conviction was quashed, I was released immediately but, overjoyed as I was to be free, I now had the problem of finding somewhere to live.

I could not return to Aberbach. For one thing it was a place with too many memories. I had been a bride there twice and lost two husbands there; for another thing, although my neighbours might smile at me, I knew they would gossip behind my back. I was stigmatised. Everyone who knew me would remember what had happened to Lance and Grant. Some folk might still believe I was a murderer. There might even be jokes made at my expense, saying I was a jinx to men—"God help the next man she marries!" I was ashamed to leave the house. You and Reg helped me out at that time, dealing with estate agents for me when I put my house up for sale.

I had no recollection of this. My parents must have kept it to themselves, not even discussing it in front of me. They knew I was always listening to their conversations, ears flapping, and decided I shouldn't know. But I remembered the day the board went up on Hazel's wall.

"Hey Mam," I said, "Hazel's moving."

"That's right."

"Where's she going to?"

"I don't know. Social services won't let her have her baby back until she has a settled home."

"Why doesn't she stay here?"

"No, it's for the best."

"Who's going to look after Freddy?" I looked at the black furry shape lying on the settee. We had taken him in while Hazel was in prison.

"I suppose he's ours now," Mam said.

"I thought you didn't like cats."

"Well, I can't throw him out on the street, can I?"

I marvelled at the fact my parents had taken to the kitten so quickly, even to the point of allowing him on the furniture—something my mother had been dead against when she took him in. He only had to rub around her legs in the kitchen, purring, and she became putty in his paws. Wonders would never cease!

I smiled at this fond recollection and resumed reading.

Social services helped me out and found me a

flat in Cardiff. With the sale of the house in Cwm Terrace and Lance's insurance, I was able to set up home. The flat was part of what had once been a quite substantial house and was in a quiet, leafy street in a suburb not far from where I had lived with Lance. There was a couple in the flat above, and I had the ground floor. I bought a few sticks of furniture from a nearby antique/junk shop; I had the pouffe and picture Lance had bought me and all my pots and pans and china, table and chairs from the house in Aberbach. I left Grant's washing machine behind and bought a new one. I hired a man with a van, and we moved most of the stuff very early one morning before most of the nosy neighbours were up and about.

The flat had been recently painted before it was put up for sale. I could still smell the fresh paint. There was a bay window at the front and I put up net curtains. The place was light and airy, and I thought it would suit me well. The only worry I had right then was how I was going to manage financially. I would have to find a job, and that meant finding a nursery, crèche or childminder for my baby. I discussed this with my social worker— her name was Diane. She said she would look into it, but for the time being my maternity grant would tide me over.

Then she brought Marianne to me. A district nurse visited me a few times to show me how to feed and bath my baby. She also left me a book by Dr Spock on how to bring up children and a box full of goodies—baby oil, nappies, talcum powder, some tins of baby food, a jar of Virol, a pot of Vaseline and some leaflets. Diane had already given me a Milton sterilising unit and some baby clothes. I suppose I should have been grateful to them for their help, but as soon as Marianne was returned to me, things started going wrong.

Although Marianne was the third baby I had given birth to, I had never actually looked after one on a daily basis. I was quite lonely at the time, scared, not sure of myself, and worried about money. I had not met any of my new neighbours. The couple upstairs worked and were out all day. There was an older lady next door, apparently—a widow like me—but I had never seen her. I wondered if I had done the right thing in moving there. Despite my comfortable surroundings, I was homesick for Aberbach and my nosy but kind-hearted neighbours. If I had not been so hasty to run away, I could have counted on you and some of the other people in the street to help me look after my child. As it was, I could not cope. I was not used to babies, and Marianne seemed to cry a lot.

Sometimes she would not go to sleep or she woke during the night, and then—although I fed her, changed her and nursed her—she would not go back to sleep. Sometimes I joined her and cried myself. I was so tired. When the district nurse's visits ceased, I had no support and I became very low. I had never heard of 'post-natal' depression then, but I presume it was what I was suffering from.

I used to examine Marianne's tiny little face

and look for signs of Lance. I should have loved her for his sake, but I felt nothing, no bond with the infant. She was dark-haired whereas Lance was fair, and though she was so small and perhaps resembled nobody in particular at that stage, I found myself seeing a semblance of Grant's features in her little face.

I put the book down hard. So, did she have an affair with Grant? I asked my bedroom wall. Did she give in to his advances? I remembered such a phrase coming from Hazel at one of her dress fittings and smiled to think of my young self believing Grant had given her a money loan that he was forcing her to repay. But I was angry with Hazel. If she *had* slept with Grant, how could she?!

I read on.

Of course, what I could really see were my own features in my baby's face.

Oh, Hazel. Forgive me. Of course, Marianne was a miniature version of you!

One day when Marianne was sleeping, I found myself crying uncontrollably. I took some aspirin, fully intending to do away with myself. Then I looked over to the cradle where she was sleeping. She had cried so much that morning and finally she slept, at peace.

I ran to the house next door, ringing the doorbell frantically. A lady of about sixty with frizzy grey hair and glasses answered the door.

"Whatever's the matter?" she asked in quite a posh voice.

"My baby! My baby! She's stopped breathing. I think she's dead!"

"Oh. Good gracious!" the woman declared. "Shall I ring for an ambulance?"

"Yes please, I haven't got a phone. Please. Be quick!"

I waited while she dialled 999. That taken care of, she followed me into my flat, into the sitting room. I lifted the baby out of her cot. She was limp and lifeless.

"Oh dear God," the woman cried. "Have you tried the kiss of life?"

"Yes."

"Then try again!"

I lay the baby on the sofa and applied my mouth over Marianne's tiny nose and mouth. I was still trying resuscitation when the ambulance crew arrived, and then they took over. I lost track of time. I don't know how long they tried to bring Marianne back to life. Then, at last, the male paramedic sat back on his heels.

"No pulse. No breathing. I'm sorry, love—there's no sign of life. I'm afraid the baby's gone."

The other paramedic was a woman. She spoke with some authority, and she worried me. "Can you tell us exactly what happened, Mrs…?"

"Taylor. I put the baby to sleep in her cot, and the next thing I knew… the next thing I knew… I could see she wasn't breathing. And then I panicked and went next door for Mrs…"

"Matthews."

"Matthews."

The woman paramedic was writing. "About how long ago was that, my love?"

"I'm not sure…"

"About what time did you notice the baby wasn't breathing?"

I looked at Mrs Matthews. She seemed to be in shock.

"I can't remember. What time did I come around to you?"

"I'm not sure of the time. I rang the emergency number straight away."

"They'll have a record of the time the call was made. And how was the baby when you arrived?"

Mrs Matthews was white. "Like she is now— no signs of life. Mrs Taylor kept giving her the kiss of life till you arrived."

The paramedic turned to me. "Had you tried mouth to mouth resuscitation previously before seeking help?"

"Yes."

"Any other form of resuscitation? Massaging the heart?"

"No. I was afraid to hurt her."

Why was she questioning me so severely?

Mrs Matthews thought the same. "Do you have to ask all these questions? This poor woman's just lost her baby."

"I'm afraid we have to, Mrs Matthews. The police will ask the same questions."

"The police?" we chorused.

"I'm afraid the police have to be informed in the case of any sudden unexplained death."

While we were answering her questions, the male paramedic was wrapping the baby blanket around Marianne and picking her up tenderly. "I'm afraid we have to take the baby away for an autopsy to be performed to ascertain cause of death."

"No!" I cried.

Mrs Matthews put her arm around me protectively.

"Can you stay with her for a while?" asked the woman paramedic.

"Certainly."

After they left, Mrs Matthews made me a cup of tea. "I've put three sugars in it—they say it's good for shock."

I was so glad of her maternal busyness.

"When can I see my baby?" I asked, dry-eyed.

"I don't know, dear. They'll let you know, I'm sure. There'll be the funeral to arrange and that…" She sighed. "It's on the increase, you know. Cot death. No one knows what causes it."

A doctor called and gave me a sedative to take. I put the pills to one side. I had taken aspirins not long before and didn't know how they would react with them.

A policeman arrived. With a notebook. He asked the same questions as the paramedic had and then some more. He wanted to know about the baby's feeds. When was the last one? Had the baby gone to sleep immediately after her feed? Had she been sick? He wanted to know if Marianne had cried a lot that day.

"No more than usual."

"Did she usually cry a lot?"

"Sometimes."

"Do you think she cried in a different way?"

"What do you mean?"

"Did the baby seem more distressed than usual?"

"No."

Then he wanted to know how I had placed the baby in the cot to sleep. He asked if I had consumed any alcohol recently. If I had a pet in the house. So many questions. I felt exhausted. After he left, I was sick in the kitchen sink.

The post-mortem found no obvious cause of death. I tried not to think of what they had done to that little body to determine what had killed it. It was classed as a "probable cot death. Cause unknown."

I had made a new friend in my neighbour, Mrs Matthews. She had been loath to leave me alone, but I was glad when they all left. I felt peaceful then. She was very kind to me, calling round regularly to see how I was coping.

"So recently widowed, and now to lose your baby. Och, it's a sad burden you have to bear at such a young age."

Hazel was only twenty-six years old. So much had happened to her during her young life.

I put the diary down, then picked it back up again. Had I read it correctly? I re-read the last couple of pages. Did Hazel just admit to killing her own baby? I read her words over and over. It was not said outright, but I was sure that's what she meant.

...finally she slept, at peace.

I tried to picture the scenario. Hazel had had a trying day with a crying baby. Depressed, she had intended to take her own life. She smothered the child, probably with a pillow or a cushion, then took an overdose but could not go through with it and panicked. She evidently had not taken enough aspirin to kill herself, only enough to make herself sick. And once she had vomited, her stomach was clear of the drug. Was that what happened?

So Rachel was not Marianne; Marianne was dead. Who was the Rachel I knew then? Was she the Rachel who had been adopted—in other words, Grant's child? Was that why Hazel had given her a photograph of Grant as her father? Why then did she know him as Lance? And if Rachel was the Rachel who had been adopted— God, this was getting confusing!—how did Hazel get her back?

What a can of worms I had opened! Hazel, what a mess your life was. Why had I been dragged into all of this?

I thought I had forgotten the lady who had lived two doors down from us in Aberbach. The lady who had lost two husbands in quick succession. Obviously, she had been there in the back of my mind all the time, which was why I had named my novel's heroine Hazel. It was only when Sue pointed out to me that she remembered a woman called Hazel that I started having flashbacks and decided I wanted to know more about what had happened to that poor woman.

And now I wished I had left well alone.

***

I told Gerry what I had read. He took it calmly.

"Are you sure you're not reading into it what you want to believe? You and your over-dramatic mind. You've always thought of Hazel as a mystery to be solved. Yes, her life was a very complicated one; yes, life threw its fair share of shit at her. She also made some rash and ill-judged decisions and got herself into some serious pickles. But a child murderer?"

I bristled. "She lied to my parents about when she first met Grant. They thought she met him for the first time after Lance's death. Then, did she lie about the paternity of Marianne? It could be that she killed the child because she did not know if the father was Lance or Grant. And she got away with it, Gerry. She got away with it."

"If she did kill Marianne—*if*—she was depressed. She had post-natal depression. But there is no proof she did." He sighed.

I was in full flow. "And come to that, was Grant's death really an accident? Did she mean to push him into the path of the train deliberately?"

"Oh, come on!"

"No. Has she been pulling the wool over our eyes all along?"

He gave up and shrugged. "Believe what you will, then."

CHAPTER TWENTY-NINE

We had a short holiday in Yorkshire, staying with friends, and I was glad to get Hazel and all her problems out of my hair. I never thought it would, but reading the diaries had brought me down. Gerry hated to see me miserable. It was his suggestion that we have a short break, and I rang my friend Joan to see if it was convenient to stay with her. We had first met at teacher training college and then she had moved to the Dales where her parents still lived—very old now but still independent.

Gerry and I loved the Yorkshire Dales. The scenery was breathtaking, and somehow the very air was different. Fresher. My friend and her husband were hospitable and kind. I wished she had not moved so far away from me; I realised how much I missed her. It was very tempting to discuss Hazel with her, but Gerry told me, "No Hazel. No dredging up old memories. Forget her for a week at least, can't you?"

I obeyed. I wanted to visit Haworth again. It was many years since I had been to the Brontes' old home. And we visited Harrogate and had to take tea in Betty's Tea Shop, of course. Gerry wanted to go to the Railway Museum in York, and I was determined to see Harlow Carr Gardens again. Joan's husband, Brian, had retired and was happy to drive us around, and I had some pleasant walks with Joan and her dog, Bowler, while the men watched railway DVDs.

Though it was spring there was warmth in the sun, and we returned home with colour in our cheeks, feeling happy and silly. A mound of mail lay on the dining table where Daniel had left it for us. I checked the messages on the answer phone. "Four new messages and two saved messages." I listened to the new ones.

My daughter Sarah, back from a holiday in Spain. "What more have you uncovered, Mum? Let me know. We're fine. All's well. Speak to you soon."

A message from daughter number two, Chloe. "Hi Mum, won't be home for a while. Chicken pox and glandular fever doing the rounds here. I don't want to bring any bugs home. Have I had either of them? I can't remember. Let me know. I guess you and Dad are off gallivanting. Give us a ring when you get back."

Then a message from Rachel. "Hi Siân, it's Rachel. I'd really like to see those letters from my grandmother. Can you let me have them soon? If they'll cost too much to send, let me know and I'll drop by to pick them up."

She sounded quite reasonable this time. *Drat!* I had really wanted to finish reading Hazel's diary before I gave up the letters. Then I could decide exactly how much to tell Rachel of her mother's history. But after the last reading session, I was not sure I wanted to tell her anything. Like Gerry had said, "Let sleeping dogs lie." I wasn't sure I wanted to read any more of Hazel's revelations myself.

The last message was another one from Rachel. She sounded both resigned and irritated, if it's possible to convey both feelings in such a short message.

"Hi Siân. It's Rachel again. I left you a message a couple of days ago. You've probably gone away, or maybe you don't want to answer. When you pick up this message, can you get in touch please?"

I phoned both my daughters. Sarah was at work, so I left her a message on *her* answer phone. We had times like that when it seemed impossible to catch each other at home.

Chloe had succumbed to chicken pox and was covered in spots. She said her boyfriend Lee had it too. I didn't know there *was* a regular boyfriend, so this was news to me. I sympathised with her, advised camomile lotion to relieve the itching, confirmed that Gerry and I had both had it but wasn't sure about Dan. I said I would try and get to see her when I had ironed out a few things this end. She took it to mean I was working on my novel, and I didn't correct her.

Gerry had taken the cases upstairs and made us both a cup of tea. I took my tea up to the bedroom and began unpacking, sorting out dirty washing for the wash basket and putting unused clothes back in the chest of drawers. Toiletries went into the bathroom, and then I left the empty cases on the landing for Gerry or Daniel to take up into the loft. Then, wearily, I opened the ottoman and took out Hazel's diaries. It had to be done. I had nearly finished reading them; I could not leave this thing half done. I drank my tea and sat on the bed.

I could not stay in Cardiff. I could not go back to Aberbach. I missed the friendliness of the mining communities in the Valleys, but I did not want people to know my business. I called myself Hazel Taylor now so no one would associate me with the Hazel Chase of Grant's accident. I had seen pictures of myself in newspapers with long, straightish hair, so I had it cut and permed. I told Mrs Matthews that I could not manage on my own and was leaving to live nearer friends, old friends. She understood. She was very sympathetic.

I found a small terraced house in a village called Thomastown, in a different valley from Aberbach. Though only a few miles away as the crow flies, a mountain divided the valleys, and as people didn't travel around as much as they do today, not everybody having cars, I thought I would be safe. The money I had from the sale of the flat would tide me over till I found a little job. I hired a small removals firm to take my few pieces of furniture, and I moved at dusk.

At first, I kept myself to myself and only went out when I had to, to buy food from the nearby Indian store. They stayed open till late at night, so that's when I did most of my shopping. I was very nervous and more than once I wondered why I had come back to the Valleys. I told myself, "Give it time." No one knew Lance and me as a couple here. No one knew Grant and me as a couple. Why would people connect me with the woman who had been in the papers a year previously?

But things must have played on my mind. I started doing strange things. Mr and Mrs Patel told me I was sleepwalking and had wandered into the shop a couple of times asking for tins of tomatoes. One time I was wearing only my see-though nightdress. I was horror-struck. Then they told me I had wrecked part of the shop, throwing things about. The police had been informed, but when the Patels found out it was me, they dropped the charges.

I was terrified. I knew I had been having nightmares again, but sleepwalking was a new development. They were really kind, the Patels, and asked me if I was unhappy about something. Oh yes, I was unhappy, so unhappy. I had started dreaming about Lance. He liked tomatoes but I didn't, so I hadn't bought them for a long time. It must have been on my mind to buy some for him. I thought it was just a dream—I didn't know I had actually walked into the shop in a trance and asked for them.

I could not tell the Patels the whole truth, but their kindness unhinged me, and I confessed that I had lost two husbands in tragic circumstances. I didn't have much money and I didn't know what to do.

I thought Mrs Patel would cry, she looked so

sad. *"So young. Two husbands! To lose one is bad enough. Life has not been good to you."*

Mr Patel offered practical help. "Hazel, would you like to work for us part-time? Sometimes I have to go to the warehouse, and my wife has our son to look after and take to school. It would be good if you could mind the shop once or twice a week and we will pay you. Will that help?"

"Oh, it would, it would," I told him. I was so grateful to them.

I slept much better after that. The money would not be much, but at least I would have some income, and if I could find another little part-time job, perhaps cleaning, then I would be able to keep my head above water.

***

A woman came into the shop when I was serving behind the counter. I sold her some cigarettes. She gave me a strange look as she took them from me and I handed her the change. She continued to stare at me. My heart thumped. Perhaps she had heard about my nocturnal wanderings.

I must have appeared very haughty. "I'm sorry. Do I know you?"

"Are you Hazel?" she asked.

"Yes, and you are…?"

"Hazel, that was married to Lance Taylor?"

"Yes. He died in a motorway accident."

"I know."

"I'm sorry—I didn't catch your name."

"Avril."

"I don't think I know you."

She smiled unpleasantly. *"Well, you might not, but Lance did."*

"Oh."

Was she somehow related to my first husband? His family had come over from Australia for his funeral, but since my marriage to Grant, they had not wanted anything to do with me. Perhaps she was a distant relation. But I thought they had come from Somerset originally—I didn't know he had any relatives in the Valleys.

"Where are you living now?" she asked me.

"I lived in Cardiff for a while and then I moved here. Do you live nearby?"

"Newport. I used to live in Aberbach. I moved away a couple of years ago. I'm visiting my auntie."

"I see." She couldn't be a relative of Lance, I decided. *"Well, it's nice to have met you."*

I wanted her to go, but she continued to address me.

"I've got a little girl."

"How nice."

"But her father died and left me holding the baby."

"I'm so sorry."

"Aye."

She turned away then and left the shop. I felt faint. Someone had recognised me. Soon everyone would know who I was. People would start asking questions.

Gradually, I calmed down. She had not

mentioned Grant or the trial. Perhaps she had moved away before it all happened. She now lived in Newport. She was only visiting. Perhaps I would not see her again.

Should I move again? I did not know where to run. Perhaps I should go to London—it was easy to hide in a big city. No one would know me, and I could start all over again. I was still young. The idea took hold of me. How should I go about getting a place to live in London? I knew accommodation was expensive there; people had to have a London living allowance added to their salaries.

I would not be able to afford a house in London. What about a council house? Then, if I sold my home in Thomastown, I should have some money to live on till I found a job. Surely there would be plenty of jobs in Britain's capital city?

I went to see Cyril Thomas, the local district councillor, about how I could arrange this.

"You have your own home, I take it, Mrs Taylor?"

"Yes."

"See, if you wanted a council house in one of the London boroughs, it would have to be a transfer. You would have to be a council house tenant here."

"Oh. I didn't know that."

"Yes, yes. And then it would take some time even then, as you would have to wait for a property to become vacant. Do you mind me asking you— are your needs urgent?"

I felt defeated. "I'm running out of funds."

"And the reason why you want to move to London?"

"I have family there," I lied.

"Of course, you would stand more of a chance if you declare yourself homeless. If you sold your house here, could your family in London put you up for a while?"

I left his house, shoulders sagging. From a nearby doorway, I saw a puff of smoke. The owner of the cigarette poked her head out.

"Fancy seeing you here twice in one week. We shall have to stop meeting like this."

It was Avril. My heart sank. She looked scruffy, wearing old grubby slippers and a grey shapeless skirt.

"Oh Avril. It's you. Is this where your auntie lives?"

"Aye. I ast her if she remembered you. She does. Of course, her brain's gone funny now. She's a bit bonkers. She keeps repeating things and she forgets what day it is. She tol' me you were a murderer. You killed your husband." She laughed. "But I tol' her she was stupid, cos Lance had a car crash." She took a drag of her cigarette. "Been to see Councillor Thomas, eh?"

There was no point in denying it. Everyone knew everyone's business in the Valley communities. "Yes."

"Where you living now then?"

"Church Street."

"Oh aye."

I was anxious to get home.

"I'm off back to Newport tomorrow," she continued. "My cousin Jackie will 'ave to get someone in to look after Nora. I can't be yer all the time."

I nodded. "Elderly relatives are a big responsibility. Bye, then." I almost trotted down the street.

"Tarra, Hazel," she shouted after me.

I walked on quickly.

CHAPTER THIRTY

That evening, I had just sat down to my supper of beans on toast and a cup of tea when there came a loud banging on my front door. I opened it to see Avril. She swayed, and I could see she had been drinking. She held a terrified child by the hand.

"What is it? What is it? Come in." I wanted Avril off my doorstep. "Are you in trouble?"

She charged drunkenly down the passage into my living room, threw herself into my armchair and cackled. "You could say that!"

"Would you like a cup of tea? I've just made one."

"'Aven't you got nothing stronger?"

"No. I'm sorry."

"This"—Avril raised herself and indicated the child standing mute by the side of the chair—"is your husband's child."

My legs went beneath me. I sat down hard on my kitchen chair.

"Grant's child?"

"Grant who? No, no, no. This is your beloved Lance's kid."

"Lance?" I was confused.

"Don't give me that innocent bit! You must 'ave known."

"No, I…" I shook my head. "Lance?"

"Oh, you thought 'e only slept with me the once. Get real. You and your pernickety ways. You always thought you was above us, Miss High and Mighty. You wouldn't give him sex. He came to me."

"No, no, no. Are you a… prostitute?"

"Prostitute be buggered. I'm as decent as you—though that's not saying much. You're a murderer," she sneered. "I ast around and Auntie Nora's not wrong about that, the old bat."

"No. It was an accident. They let me go—I was acquitted."

"So you say. I've got a proposition for you."

I was in a kind of trance. I didn't answer.

"My 'usband's gone and left me. He got fed up with raising another man's kid, he said. I reckon the only way I'll get 'im back is if I get rid of her. So, I'm leaving you a present. Precious Lance's kid."

The little girl regarded us both in turn with frightened big brown eyes. She clutched a toy rabbit.

"I can't have her!" I cried. "She's your child!"

"Well, I don't want her." Avril heaved herself up out of my saggy armchair. "I'm going now. And don't dump her back on me, or I'll tell everyone around yer that you murdered your husband."

I was shocked to the core. "Lance's child?"

"You can't tell me you didn't know what your wonderful precious Lance was really like."

I shook my head. "He came back to me. He begged me to forgive him. He said he would never cheat on me again."

"Huh. He only came back to you when I tol' 'im I was up the duff," she scoffed.

"What's her name?" I asked plaintively.

"Tracy. But you can call her what you like!"

The front door slammed behind Avril. I had no idea what to do.

"Would you like a glass of milk?"

The little girl nodded.

She would not put the soft toy down but grabbed the glass out of my hand and drank the milk all in one go. Her hand was grubby. I smiled to see the moustache of milk on her upper lip. I guessed she was hungry.

My beans were congealing on the plate.

* * *

That first night, I put her to sleep in my bed. I intended to sleep in the armchair downstairs, but it was cold, so I went upstairs and crept into the bed beside her. She still clutched her rabbit in her sleep.

I lay all night listening to the rain pattering against the windowpane. What was I going to do with this child? Should I go to the police and tell them she had been left with me? The child would be taken away by social services and put into foster care. I knew all about that.

I could not believe that Lance, the man I had given my heart to, could have deceived me so badly. Or did he? I had only Avril's word that he was the father of the little girl. But what *reason did she have to lie to me? When Lance confessed to me that he had been unfaithful, was Avril the barmaid he had told me about? Or was he unfaithful to me with more than one woman? If Avril was his only mistake, could only one slip have resulted in this child? Or did he lie to me and sleep with Avril on a regular basis? But he had been so remorseful; he had cried in front of me. Lance was not the sort of man to cry. He was easy-going, hail-fellow-well-met. He was a happy man and he loved me, I knew. He left me because he could not live with the guilt he felt at betraying me. He came back because he could not live without me. Or so he said. I had believed him, and because I loved him, I forgave him and we were as we had been before. Weren't we?*

The tears ran down my cheeks. I cried silently, not wanting to wake the child. I thought I would choke.

Perhaps Avril would come back the next day and reclaim her daughter—she <u>had</u> been drunk. Perhaps she hated me because she had been jealous of my marriage to Lance. Perhaps in the cold light of day, she would come to her senses and come knocking on my door demanding the return of her child.

That did not happen.

* * *

I had very little food in the house and no clean clothes for the little girl. I took her with me into the next town. We travelled on the bus. She sat beside me in her dirty dungarees, still mute with fear, still refusing to part with her blue rabbit with the floppy ears.

In Woolworths, I bought her clothes and a doll. I could ill afford extras and spent most of my weekly budget. I would have to go without any treats such as biscuits or chocolate cake on Sunday. Perhaps I would be able to steal some food from the Patels; I would have to pretend I had been sleepwalking again. My mind was working overtime. What should I do? How could I deal with this?

When we got home, I fed the girl, bathed her and put her to bed in a clean pair of pyjamas. Then I took her grubby clothes, washed them by hand in the bath and hung them on the radiators to dry.

After a few days, I realised that Avril was not coming back and her threat had been real. She had left her child with me for good. I was stuck with her. I decided against going to the police. The child was scared enough; I did not want her traumatised further.

I wondered how old Tracy was. The clothes I had bought were for a two-year-old. She was still mute. Perhaps she could not talk yet. I thought back to when I was a two-year-old. I had been a refugee coming to Britain.

I had a vivid dream. I was with a group of children playing in the street. A man passed by in a military uniform. We instantly froze. The men in the grey uniforms were very strict. They did not like us talking or laughing too loudly, but sometimes they smiled and gave us sweets. We were playing marbles in the gutter. We must have made a noise. Another soldier opened a bedroom window and yelled at us to be quiet.

My mother told me we had to hide. Gertrude would help us. A taxi came. A stout woman in a long, dark blue coat that reached to her sensible shoes got out. She was very tall for a woman and had short, straight grey hair, most of it hidden under a navy-blue hat. An imposing figure. If she had been my nursemaid, I would never have stepped out of line.

A man appeared at the open downstairs window. "Ah, Gertrude. You are here," he said in a soft voice.

She climbed the short flight of steps, took hold of the fancy doorknob and let herself in. I followed with my mother. We walked down a short corridor and, turning to the right, found ourselves in a small parlour.

"Ah, you've arrived," someone said.

And then I woke up in a sweat, the child beside me asleep. What had I been dreaming about? I was no older than Tracy when my mother and I had gone into hiding. How were we captured? Did Gertrude betray us? Someone had betrayed us. Treachery. Lance had betrayed me. I then believed that Tracy was truly his child. Oh, Lance, Lance.

I wondered if, when Tracy grew up, she

would have flashbacks in dreams of a drunken, shouting mother who had abandoned her in a strange woman's house. Surely the child's eyes expressed fear? What had she been subjected to? I saw no injuries on her, but sometimes mental cruelty is as bad as, if not worse than, physical abuse. I would not let this child suffer any more.

I tried to converse with her. "Would you like a banana, Tracy?"

She shook her head.

"What is the name of your rabbit?"

She simply stared at me.

"He's a lovely fellow. Has he got a name?"

No response.

"Would you like me to read you a story, Tracy?"

No response.

Tracy, I did not like the name. I thought of the little girl I had had adopted. How old would she be now? About seven. I would never see her, never know where she was. Her name would have been changed. I had called her Rachel after my mother.

"I'm going to give you a new name. You're my little girl now. I'm going to call you Rachel. Do you like that name—Rachel?"

No response.

CHAPTER THIRTY-ONE

I put down the diary. So that was it! My God, the Rachel I knew wasn't even Hazel's daughter! I could not tell her this. I could not reveal that her whole life had been a deception. She would be devastated.

Thinking about Hazel's past, it was no wonder that as she aged and dementia seized her, she had become confused about Rachel and Marianne. Marianne was dead—possibly killed by her own hand—and there were two Rachels. And her dream about the babies in the cot, and then the older child who could not speak—that was a muddling up of her baby who had been born with some form of deformity and the silent little girl who had come to live with her and she brought up as her own.

I had been cross with Hazel the last time I had read her diary. Now I sympathised with her again.

* * *

Sarah called in that Friday night. She had nagged Warren into visiting his parents in Huddersfield, and he had gone off for the week. She couldn't take time off work, so she came to us for the weekend and travelled back to Birmingham on Sunday afternoon.

"So, have you finished reading Hazel's diaries, Mum? What have you discovered?"

"I've almost finished."

I told her everything. When I came to the part about Marianne's death, I read it out as Hazel had written it.

"Oh my God, Mum! Do you think she killed her baby?"

"That's the impression I got too."

"Oh my God. The poor woman. She must have been suffering from post-natal depression."

"To my mind, that doesn't excuse her from murdering her own baby."

"Mum, women do strange things at such a time. It's a known fact."

"I don't know. It seemed very premeditated to me. She was tied down with this very small baby and no means of support. With the baby out of the way, she could get back on her feet."

"I don't see it like that. She wasn't in her normal state of mind. Don't be too hard on her, Mum. She'd been through such a lot of shit, it's a wonder she *didn't* take an overdose. I wonder why she didn't go through with that?" she mused. "I suppose she was scared. She obviously didn't swallow enough pills to kill herself. I suppose when you think how hard she tried to survive…"

"I can't tell Rachel any of this."

"Certainly not. Do as I said before, Mum. Read it, then burn it."

I showed Sarah the first notebook, and we discussed things at length while Gerry and Daniel watched *Match of the Day*. I told her that Rachel had left me two messages and wanted her grandmother's letters.

"Except that she isn't her grandmother."

"Does that matter? She thinks she was. And, Mum, she will never know who her real mother was or her real grandparents. Hazel was the only mother she knew—the only family she had. This is the only identity she has. Don't take it from her."

Sarah was right. I could not leave Rachel floundering, an orphan who would never know her roots. To know the truth would bring her whole world crashing down.

"I'll let her have the letters," I decided. I would phone as soon as Sarah left us on Sunday.

However, events conspired against us. Sarah's car would not start. On Monday morning, she had to phone the library to explain what had happened, while Gerry spent the morning under the bonnet of her Ford Fiesta. Then a parcel arrived for Dan that I had to sign for. Rachel went completely out of my mind. It was late afternoon before Sarah left and I had a chance to tidy up and settle down for one of the last sessions reading Hazel's diary.

***

She wrote about another vivid dream she had.

It was night-time when we were moved, and I had no idea where I was. I could only see parts of people's faces as they were caught in torchlight: a bristling moustache, gleaming teeth, sad eyes bagged underneath. We were not allowed to speak, and our rescuers spoke very little and I could not understand them. My mother whispered that they were "Britishers" and that the language they spoke was "English". But to me they were shadowy folk, like ghosts. Unreal.

I was very hungry, and I was given a torn-off chunk of bread. We came to a large body of water and were put into a boat. I could not see how many of us there were or how long it took us to cross the water.

I sat up sweating. Was what I had dreamt an actual experience of when I was about the same age as Tracy/Rachel? It didn't fit with what I had been told before of our rescue from that terrible, grey place that smelled so bad. Was it a mixture of something I remembered and footage I had seen on television of immigrants in boats? Would images come to Rachel in dreams of another "mother" with a cigarette in her mouth and cold eyes? What would she make of them?

The child was sleeping. I touched her cheek. She stirred, then settled back into sleep.

I had other dreams. In one I was carried into a place—it looked like a large hall. I was given tasteless soup. Another little girl ate hers too quickly and vomited all over the wooden floor. Nothing was said and the mess was soon cleared up. I could not understand anything that was said to me by stout ladies in floral dresses and must have stared at them in bewilderment. My mother had been my interpreter up till then, but she had been taken away from me. She cried when they took her off on a stretcher, and I cried too, reaching out my arms to her.

One of the other refugees said to me, "Your mother is very sick. They are taking her to hospital. They will find you a home to go to. Don't worry. You will soon see your mother."

But that was the last time I ever saw her.

That time I awoke with tears on my cheeks, knowing that dream to be a direct recollection of what had really happened. It had been buried deep inside my brain. The refugee must have spoken to me in German. Strange how the brain works. I could remember nothing now of my first language.

I looked at the child. She, too, was awake, tears drying on her cheeks. Both of us had spent a restless night. I reached over and hugged her. At first she resisted, then she relaxed. And so we fell asleep again.

I became aware of a difference in the child. She began to answer to the name of Rachel. She put down her rabbit to eat a meal.

I said, "If your rabbit doesn't have a name, shall we call him Reggie? Reggie Rabbit sounds good, doesn't it?"

And the little girl smiled. Marion, I tell you— that smile melted my heart. I began to wonder if God had given me another chance to have a child of my own. This time I would take good care of it, no matter what happened. And so I picked up the fragile threads of my life and carried on. I had something to live for now. I was happier than I had been for a long time.

No one in Thomastown questioned that she was mine. She was dark-haired like me—like her mother. I had the occasional "I didn't know you had a little girl, Mrs Taylor." I told them that the child had been in the care of social services until I had got settled in my new home. Now that I had a roof over my head and a part-time job, they had allowed me to have her home. They had no reason to suspect I was not telling the truth.

Rachel, number two, grew to trust me, and as she learned to speak properly she began to call me Mum. The first time she said it, I thought my heart would burst. I bought her a little bed and a pretty rug and put her in a bedroom of her own. She began to play with the toys I bought her, and we went shopping for more clothes and new shoes, for hers had started to pinch her toes.

The Patels were kind to me and gave me more hours in the shop and allowed me to have my little girl with me. Rachel was very shy and most of the time sat quietly on a stool, talking to her dolly and sucking on the sweets or lollipops that Mrs Patel said I could give her.

I sang as I swept the floor and shook the rugs. I sang as I pegged out the washing. I joined the ladies' choir in the village, taking Rachel with me. She sat in the corner watching us and listening to us sing, and she was fussed over by the other women. My dreams and nightmares ceased and I wandered no more at night.

Avril's aunt died. I saw Avril walking along the street one day, fag in mouth as usual, and my heart nearly stopped beating. Was she going to come and take my Rachel away? How would I explain that? I turned my back on her and walked the other way.

She came to my house late at night. Bang! Bang! Bang! *I knew it was her. I did not answer.* Bang! Bang! Bang! *Louder this time. I could ignore it no longer; she would wake up the neighbours. I let her in with my finger to my lips.*

"How is she?" She threw herself into my collapsed easy chair.

"Fine. Would you like a cup of tea?"

"No. I'm not staying. I just came to tell you things are all right with me and Andy now, so you can keep the kid. You 'ave still got 'er, 'ave you?"

"Of course."

"Good. I've 'eard people say as you 'ad a little girl. Well, you'll give 'er a better life than I could, I don't doubt."

"I don't know. I have a problem…"

"What? Don't ast me for no money. I 'aven't got no money. You're not gonna blackmail me!"

"No, no, no, no. It's just that I haven't got a birth certificate for her. She'll need one for certain things, won't she, as she grows up?"

"Oh that. I've got one somewhere. I'll send it to you through the post." She heaved herself out of the chair. "You need to get some more furniture. This chair's 'ad it."

"I haven't got much money coming in. It will

have to do for now. I've got other things on my mind."

She smiled. I disliked that smile. "Yes, I s'pose you 'ave. Well, don't worry—you won't be seeing me no more. Andy and I are moving up to Coventry. 'E's got a job up there and Auntie Nora left me some money, so we're off."

I saw her to the door and leaned against it. Exhausted.

* * *

I received the birth certificate through the post. Strangely enough, she sent me a short note with it and some money. Twenty pounds. I was stunned.

Her letter read:

"You're not a bad sort, Hazel Taylor, after all. I thought you was so prim and proper, and you had Lance and I was left with his kid and he would not admit it was his, so I didn't know where to turn. I knew people was talking about me behind my back. Then Andy and I got together, but he didn't want no kid what wasn't his. When I saw you I decided you should have the upkeep of looking after Lance's kid. Not many women would take what I done to you, dumping Tracy on you like that. But you never come back at me and you never told no one what I did. Andy and I are going away, and I hope we can make a go of it. I think you like the girl. You'll be alright. Here's some money from what Auntie Nora left me. You can buy a new chair with it. Good luck. Avril."

She felt guilty for leaving her child. This was hush money. But there was no love expressed for her little girl. I put the money safe in a pot on the mantelpiece and decided I would only take half of it. I wanted to put by some money for Tracy—no, Rachel. I must always think of her as Rachel now.

I looked at the birth certificate. The father's name was Lance Taylor, sure enough. The little girl's birthday was the 5ᵗʰ June 1967. I now had a date on which to celebrate her birthday. I decided that I would buy her a good present—a pram for her dolly. And I would bake a cake and she could blow out the candles. Like a normal child. Like my child.

The name of the mother—Avril Jones. That was a problem. I traced it on to some paper and then spent hours learning how to change it to Hazel Joseph. I had learned that my real surname had been Joseph. All my life, I had thought that my name was Hannah Elizabeth Hezekiah, but I had found that Hezekiah was my father's name and that I had taken his name. My father's father's name had been Joseph, so that was his name— Hezekiah bar Joseph. Confusing. It was easier to change Jones to Joseph anyway.

Fancy that! Perhaps Hazel had made the same enquiries as I had. Perhaps she'd also made the same journey to her mother's grave.

I was intrigued by the changing of the birth certificate. I went through the same process as Hazel and spent some time trying to change the name Avril Jones to Hazel Joseph. It could be done—just. Presumably she made it a bit smudged and went over some of the other entries to make it look as if the registrar had a heavy hand.

Wow! *Hazel, you never cease to amaze me,* I thought. That must have been the last of her secrets. There was nothing more she could reveal, surely?

CHAPTER THIRTY-TWO

Rachel grew in stature and confidence. I really began to think she was mine. At four years old, she went to nursery class in the village school. She was a bright child. As well as working part-time in the Patels' shop, I became a cleaner in the school and occasionally I typed letters for people, glad to put my secretarial skills to use. Every so often, a cheque would arrive through the post. I opened a bank account and put Avril's money in it for Rachel. I did not touch a penny of it.

Then, one day, a short skinny man with thinning hair came into the Patels' shop for cigarettes. He told me his name was Carl and he was Avril Jones's brother. I did not like the sneer on his face. I knew that he knew. He told me he was moving into his auntie's house. How long would it be before he let the cat out of the bag? Time to move on, Hazel.

I moved back to Cardiff. First, I rented an awful house in Roath, then I moved to Llanishen. I managed to get a job in the Inland Revenue Offices. Anxious not to lose Avril's 'hush money', both times I had my mail redirected. After a couple of years, the cheques ceased, but by then I did not need her money and I contributed to Rachel's 'fund' from my own wages.

Rachel did not adjust to the moves well, but she was a very able pupil and her schooling was not affected. Each time we moved house, she became a little withdrawn, and I was anxious to please her and praise her to draw her out and make her happy.

By this time, I realised she was a serious young soul, and there was a sort of rift between us that possibly could never be entirely healed. I did not know what to expect from a child. If I had thought she would be eternally grateful to me for looking after her, that was folly on my part. She took my care for her for granted. Perhaps all children do of their natural parents. I would not know.

Marion, I wish that my life had been different, but I have tried to make the best of it. I never remarried or looked at other men in a romantic or sexual way. I had loved two men and been disappointed in both. I had grieved for the one I loved dearly, only to find he was not the man I thought he was. I had been loved by another who could not hold his temper, and I caused him to die.

All in all, I had had my fill of men. I had lost three children and then God had given me one last chance to be a proper mother. I concentrated all my efforts on bringing up Rachel.

After we moved to Llanishen, my life was pretty uneventful. Rachel is almost grown up now. She is starting university in the autumn and I am very proud of her. I think of her as my own daughter, and I don't think I could love her more if she was.

She is still a serious, sometimes severe person, and our relationship can get strained at times, but that is her nature and I can't change it. She only knows me as her mother. Someday she may wish to know the truth. I cannot tell her face to face. I don't know what to do for the best. Some people would say it is her right to know the truth about her origins, but I would not want her to be hurt. Similarly, I do not know if it would be right to tell her my history. I decided to write it all down.

I am leaving this diary to you, Marion. You will know what to do for the best, whether to tell Rachel who she really is—and who I really am. You were always very wise, Marion. You will do the best for her.

And there, the bulk of Hazel's diary ended. There was just a postscript at the end, written some years later.

Dear Marion,

I am so afraid I am losing my mind as my poor dear mother did. My dreams and nightmares are back, and sometimes they seem more real than real life. I have kept my diaries secreted among my personal things, but in case I do succumb to dementia and I am taken away, I am leaving them, along with my mother's letters and some photographs, with the solicitors James, Jenkins and Paget with instructions that they be given to you in the event of my death. Or if you have predeceased me, I would like them to go to your daughter, Siân, who was always such a bright, sparky girl. And hopefully, she will know what to do with them.

Sighing, I closed the book. So there it was. All the mysteries solved. But what should I do with all this information?

I packed up Rachel Senior's letters and some of the photographs and took them to Rachel's house.

She lived in a large house in Cyncoed, a well-to-do part of Cardiff. Appropriately enough, it was inhabited by solicitors, lawyers, doctors and other professionals, many of them Jewish. There were two cars in the drive; one was Rachel's BMW and one was a silver Jaguar I presumed was her husband's, so they were both at home.

Rachel came to the door.

"Oh. You didn't answer my message."

"Sorry. We've been on holiday."

She wasn't going to invite me in. I smelled something cooking, a wonderful aroma of garlic and tomatoes. I wondered if they were having spaghetti bolognese. My stomach rumbled.

"I've brought you the letters."

"Have you read them?"

"Yes." I hesitated. "I've also brought you some photographs, but I've no idea who the people are."

She held out her hand and I gave her the parcel. And then she moved back into the hallway, starting to close the glass-panelled door. I realised I was being dismissed. Oh well— we were not friends. All we had in common was Hazel, and now she was gone. I had a husband

and son to cook for, so I had better go home and see to them. By the time I caught the train, it would be quite late. I hoped my menfolk would have cooked or been to the chippie.

I sort-of waved as I walked down the drive and I heard Rachel's door close. Firmly. That was the end of that then. I would not see her again.

As the train took me homewards, I tussled with my thoughts. I walked down the hill towards my house, deciding I would do as Sarah had suggested and burn the diaries.

But as I was peeling potatoes for a late dinner, I changed my mind again.

"Can't we have chips?" grumbled Daniel. "I'm starving. My stomach thinks my throat's been cut."

"I've peeled the spuds now. Dinner won't be long. Do me a favour, honeybunch, and get the loft ladder down."

"Only if we can have steak."

"It's already in the pan."

I re-wrapped the diaries and handed them up to Dan. "Put this in the old trunk. It's not locked."

"It's cold up here. Good Lord, what a lot of junk. You haven't still got my old tricycle! Why on earth didn't you give it away?"

"I'd forgotten about that. I'll keep it for Sarah's children, if she has any. Come on down now, Dan, don't start poking about up there. Hell, I can hear the meat spitting. Your dinner's almost done."

CHAPTER THIRTY-THREE

And up in the attic Hazel's diaries stayed. I could not let Rachel have them. But something stopped me destroying them.

I finished writing my story about a woman called Harriet. It had turned into what people today call a romcom. I'd had no idea of how it would develop when I began it. I sent it off to a publishing house and awaited their response in trepidation.

My daughter Sarah announced that she and Warren were getting married. There was no engagement because they had been living together for two years. Daniel decided that he and his on-off girlfriend, Samantha, should finally set up home together, and moved out.

Sarah didn't involve me in her wedding plans; she and Warren didn't want a big, fussy wedding, but all the same, I found myself suddenly interested in wedding gowns and mother-of-the-bride outfits. Two days after I had made up my mind on what I should wear and ordered an outfit from the JD Williams catalogue, the phone rang.

"Siân, its Rachel. Are you busy?"

"Not really. I've just put my feet up in front of the telly. I've spent the last few days shopping for wedding stuff—my daughter's getting married."

"Is your husband around?"

"He is. But I can always send him down the pub." I sensed she wanted to see me. "Is it urgent?"

"Is it all right if I call round?"

"Yes. What's wrong?"

"Something weird. I can't discuss it on the phone. Can I come round now? I'm parked up. I'm only ten minutes from you."

"I'll put the kettle on."

She sounded upset. It had been a couple of months since I gave her the letters and photographs. Had something about them disturbed her so much that she had to ask me about them? Was it the photographs of the babies? I wondered if I had done right in giving them to her.

I opened the door to a pale-faced Rachel.

"Come in. I've made tea."

She sat down on the sofa as if in a trance.

"You said something weird has happened?" I coaxed her.

"Yes. I wondered if there was anything else in my mother's parcel that could shed light on it. Perhaps something you held back from me?"

I shook my head, not about to reveal the existence of anything else at this juncture. "Why? What's happened?"

"The most awful thing. We had a fire. There was a fault with the electric cooker. A teacloth had been left on the ring, it caught fire, one thing led to another… We were all out. Came home to find my house in flames. Siân, it's awful. My home…" She burst into tears.

"Oh no," I gasped. "How terrible! What will you do?"

She sobbed for a while. I rushed to get her a handkerchief and brought in the tea on a tray. She composed herself.

"We have insurance, of course, and we have savings. We have a caravan in west Wales and a holiday home in Spain. We're not destitute. But it was still such an awful shock. I've lost so many personal things."

"I'm sure it was. I don't know how I would cope."

"And the parcel you gave me. All my grandmother's letters, the photographs you gave me, along with all my own photos, documents, receipts, bank statements, my own letters—all destroyed." She sniffed. "I should have put them in metal files and cabinets, I know that now, but some things were left lying around or in cardboard files in my bedroom. I've had to contact building societies, banks; I've had to replace all sorts of things—passports, driving licences—you wouldn't believe all the stress I've had."

"Oh, believe me, I would. I couldn't imagine losing everything in a fire like that and losing my home. It must be dreadful. I would be stressed out of my head."

Rachel took a sip of tea. I had put out my best china cups and saucers in her honour.

"The thing is…." Rachel started.

I waited.

"The thing is, I had to apply to Somerset

House for new birth certificates for all of us..."

I waited.

"And they sent me this." She reached inside her handbag and produced a form. "I can't understand." She handed it to me. I knew what was coming. "According to this, my mother is Avril Jones. That's not another of Hazel's pseudonyms, is it?"

"No."

"So Hazel was not my mother?"

I could not save her from the truth.

"No."

She was angry now and had two vivid pink spots on her cheeks.

"So who the hell was, or is, Avril Jones?"

"She was Lance Taylor's lover."

"Lance, the godlike Lance? I take it he *was* my father?"

"Yes."

"Are you telling me I'm illegitimate?"

"Yes."

I felt a sinking feeling in my stomach. I had wanted to spare her from this. So had Hazel.

"How the hell do you know all this, and why didn't you tell me?"

Oh Hazel. Hazel. God grant me the wisdom you thought I had.

"Hazel was very good friends with my mother, as you know. My mother told me," I lied. "And I promised not to tell anyone—ever."

"What happened to my real mother?"

"After Lance died, there were two women

grieving: his rightful wife, Hazel, and the mother of his little girl—you—Avril. Avril could not cope on her own, so Hazel stepped in and adopted you."

"I've never seen any adoption papers."

"Perhaps Hazel destroyed them."

"Why would she do that? Why didn't she tell me when I grew old enough to know?"

"She looked upon you as her own. She was always afraid that Avril would want you back. She couldn't give you up, so she moved to Cardiff from Thomastown."

"I was born where—Thomastown?"

"Here in Aberbach."

"Aberbach. I didn't know my mother lived here."

"Well, she did once. You were born there. Probably in the front bedroom of Avril Jones's house."

"Wasn't there a scandal? Didn't people know?"

"Her family probably closed ranks. And I don't think Avril would have cared—she wasn't sensitive like Hazel."

"What are you saying? That she was common?"

I didn't answer.

"My God!" Rachel was having difficulty getting her head around these facts. Something came into her mind. "This Marianne you're always asking about. Who was she?"

"She was your half-sister. Hazel and Lance's daughter. I think she must have died as a baby.

Hazel must have thought God had sent you to replace her. That makes sense, doesn't it, Rachel? I think that's why at the end of her life she was getting a bit mixed up between the two of you."

Rachel's eyes narrowed. "How do you know this now when you didn't before?"

"I just worked it out from what my mother told me about Avril's baby. I didn't know your name was Rachel; Avril called you Tracy."

We sat in silence for a while, both lost in thought. I offered her a fresh cup of tea but she declined. I thought that all in all I had made a good fist of inventing a plausible story to account for the way in which Rachel had become Hazel's daughter. A bit vague but mostly true.

"The birth certificate I'd seen before… My full name was written as "Rachel Tracy", but…"

"Hazel doctored it, I suppose, so you wouldn't ask questions. She wanted you to believe she was your real mother."

"But I used that as a proof of my identity more than once!"

Yes—and she worked for the law.

"I don't suppose people examine them very closely. As long as you produce something looking like a certificate, employers and others don't scrutinise them thoroughly, and if Hazel smudged it or something…" I patted her knee. "What's done is done. You didn't break the law."

"Not knowingly, I didn't." She moved her knee away. "But ignorance is no defence in law."

"More fool the law. Look, no one will know about

the dodgy document now. It's been destroyed."

The front door opened and two tipsy men arrived, making a lot of noise.

"Oh, sorry," Gerry said, seeing Rachel sitting on the sofa. "I didn't realise we had company. Ssh!" he warned Daniel, who was singing out of tune. Both men looked sheepish.

"Look at the state of you both!" I scolded. "Dan, what are you doing here? You don't live here any longer."

"She won't let me in like this," he whined. "Can't I crash out on the sofa tonight?"

"The bed's still made up in your old room. Get a proper night's sleep."

Rachel had jumped up. "Is that the time? I must be going. We're staying with friends—I mustn't keep them up."

"Is this your coat?" Gerry handed her a fur jacket draped across the back of the sofa.

"Thank you." Rachel took it from him and put it on.

I went with her to the front door.

"Look, don't blame Hazel," I said awkwardly. "She really loved you and thought of herself as your mother. She didn't want you to be stigmatised."

"As illegitimate. A bastard."

"Don't use that term, Rachel. Hazel loved you and brought you up the best she could. No one else knows about the truth of your birth," I lied. "They're all dead now. And no one else needs to know."

"But *I* know."

I felt exasperated. "What difference does it make now? They're all dead – Hazel, Lance, probably Avril. It's all in the past. Let it go. You're still you—Rachel Taylor, that is. Nothing changes who you are, what you are. Do you remember Hazel's words that you quoted at the funeral? 'If tragedy befalls us, we must endure it. If obstacles arise, we must surmount them.' You have just lost your home in a fire. What is important now is getting your family back on its feet. Forget Hazel. Forget Avril. What matters is you and your family."

She leaned over and kissed me on the cheek. "Thank you, Siân. I must put things into perspective, mustn't I? It's just… There's been so many shocks. I have a lot to thank you for, not least for keeping Hazel's secret." She searched my face. "If you find out anything else… Could I ask you to keep her—and mine too, now—secret again? Can I trust you?"

I nodded. "Forever."

I walked back into my sitting room. Daniel had gone to bed and Gerry had put the television on. I told him all that had transpired between Rachel and me.

Totally sober now, Gerry said, "I suppose this wasn't the right time to tell her there's another Rachel out there somewhere?"

"She must never know. Like you said before, Gerry, everyone has secrets."

When I went to bed, I could not sleep. I thought of Rachel and her family losing their lovely home to a fire and how lucky they were not to have been burnt alive in their beds. I mused over everything I had discovered about Hazel. One thing that bothered me was why she had told Rachel her father was Lance Taylor but then showed her a picture of Grant Chase.

CHAPTER THIRTY-FOUR

I had a dream that night. I stood outside a burning building. I watched the orange flames but was turned to stone. Then a figure came out of the fire. She had a beaky nose and curly hair. I thought she was a witch.

"You've killed me! You've killed me!" she cried.

As she raised her long fingers, talons ready to scratch out my eyes, we both heard a baby cry. The witch turned round; her hair with a fiery halo. A man emerged from the inferno, carrying a baby.

I knew it was Lance, but the witch called out, "It's Grant! He loves me."

"It's your baby!" I shouted in response.

"Not mine!"

I awoke in a bath of sweat and had to go to the bathroom. I washed my face with cold water and mopped my bare arms with a cool flannel.

I told Gerry about my dream the next morning and asked him why Hazel had shown Rachel a photograph of Grant Chase and told her it was Lance.

"She probably didn't have one of Lance," he suggested, "so she just showed her one of Grant. After all, Rachel had never known Grant. She never knew it wasn't a photo of her father."

Of course, it sounded so simple when he said it.

***

I had a few more strange dreams. I wondered about going to see my GP and asking him for some sleeping tablets, but Gerry told me it was only because my mind was so full of Hazel and her history.

"You've been poring over the diaries and it's upset your mind. It's time you forgot about Hazel and her problems. Like you told Rachel, it's all in the past. Let it go."

He's right. He's always right. Why couldn't Hazel have found a husband like mine? She deserved some happiness in her life. Perhaps she found a sort of peace in bringing up Rachel, but she obviously never had complete peace of mind, hence all her dreams and nightmares. She could never utterly forget how her mother died, her abusive foster parent, the children she had lost and the deaths of her two husbands.

***

I bumped into an old school friend of mine called Phyllis. She had been in the same class as me, and I thought she was the font of all knowledge simply because she seemed to know all about S-E-X when I was very naïve and knew very little. She had moved to Birmingham many years ago. She was only visiting Aberbach to attend a cousin's funeral, and when we cast eyes on each other, we were both unsure at first. We were both grey now and she wore glasses.

After deciding it was really me, she whooped, "Siân Watkins, as I live and breathe! How long has it been? Where are your plaits?"

I, too, was overjoyed. "Good Lord! Phyllis. Is it really you after all this time?"

She told me the funeral was the next morning and she and her husband would be travelling back to the Midlands in the evening. So it was decided that we had to seize the moment and went to a café for a long lunch and catch-up.

We boasted about our children's achievements, and she showed me pictures of her grandchildren as we waited for our toasted sandwiches.

"How many do you have?"

"None." I sighed. "I'm afraid my children are slow getting around to it."

"Oh you will, you will," she said. "And you won't know yourself when you're a grandma. Nice thing is you can borrow them and give them back when you've had enough." She laughed her dirty laugh that always got me going.

Over our meal and coffees, we reminisced of days gone by, and the other customers in the café must have wondered at us as we giggled and spluttered over some of our memories.

"I wonder what became of Celia Jones?" Phyllis said. "Everyone knew the baby was hers, but the family closed ranks and passed it off as her mother's."

I felt a cold shiver down my spine.

Phyllis carried on talking and laughing. "Do you remember Margie Phillips who only had one arm? Yet there was nothing she couldn't do. Remember Dai Shortfall? God knows how he got that name. Everyone had nicknames then, didn't they? Remember Mr Murphy with the cross-eyes? He used to frighten me. If I saw him walking towards me, down the lane I'd run like hell."

I recovered myself. "I remember your mam chasing your dad down the street with a saucepan…"

"Because he'd come home drunk!"

"Do you remember…?"

"Do you remember…?"

Little snapshots of memories came into our brains, almost as vivid as the day the incidents occurred. All the time I was thinking, *Don't say it!* But she did.

"Do you remember Hazel?"

I stopped laughing. "She died."

"Well, I expect she would have by now. Still, she wouldn't have been all that old."

"She had Alzheimer's and she was in a home."

"There's a lot of it about. We didn't have that name for it in the old days. We used to call it senile dementia," she chattered on.

"She got a bit muddled."

"I'm getting that way myself." She didn't notice

that the laughter had gone out of me.

"I met her daughter, Rachel. Her house burned down."

"Whose? Rachel's? How awful. Was anyone injured?"

"No, no. They were all at work. She's okay. They stayed with friends for a bit, then rented till the insurances came through. I think they're all right now. She lives in Cyncoed."

"Moneyed, eh. Hazel must have done all right for herself then."

Had she forgotten Lance, Grant, the trial?

"She had a hard life. She lost two husbands."

"Ah yes. I seem to remember. There was something strange about the one husband's death, wasn't there?"

"He fell under a train."

She shuddered. "Not a nice way to go. She was a bit strange—wasn't she, old Hazel?"

"In what way?"

"I don't know, really. I can't remember. I think my mother stopped speaking to her at one time. Said she was a tramp. Was she?"

"Oh no, not Hazel. She had a sad life. She was good friends with my mam and dad."

"I remember Marion and Reg—staunch chapelgoers. What happened to your brother, Brian?"

The moment had passed.

We finished our meal and paid the bill. I told her Sarah was living in Birmingham, too, and she said she would pop in to the library and introduce herself. We swapped addresses and home numbers and promised to keep in touch.

* * *

I dreamed that night of a young man with a round head. He was bald, skinny and his skin was smooth and shiny. By his side was a young woman dressed in a purple sari, her hair braided. I knew the man. What was his name?

The woman smiled shyly. I didn't know her.

"Have you destroyed the evidence?" The round-headed man asked me.

"No."

He smiled. "Perhaps you ought to write your own version."

"There is only *one* version."

"Is there? Nothing is as it seems."

The next day, Gerry went up into the attic and retrieved Hazel's diaries. He soon had a fire blazing in a galvanised bucket in the backyard. We stood in the drizzle and watched Hazel's life go up in smoke.

EPILOGUE

May 2016

Yesterday, Sarah told me she was expecting her first child. I was ecstatic.

"Boy or girl?"

"We don't want to know. We want it to be a surprise."

"Okay." In my day you didn't know until the birth anyway.

I was so happy. Daniel and Samantha had decided to get married that summer. At last. Two settled, only Chloe to go.

After Sarah's phone call, I went straight out and bought some baby clothes in Mothercare in Cardiff. I was flush because my novel had been accepted for publication. Yesterday was one of the best days of my life.

I called in the corner shop on my way home and picked up a hand of bananas, some biscuits and a *South Wales Echo*. At home, I made myself a cup of tea, kicked off my shoes and settled in my armchair to look at the *Echo*. For some reason, I always read a newspaper back to front and start with the Births, Marriages and Deaths.

What a shock I received to read:

APRIL 29TH

The sudden death is announced of Rachel Betts (née Taylor) at the age of 49. Dearly beloved wife of Leonard, beloved mother of Holly and Gareth…

There was a short piece inside the main body of the paper.

Sudden Death of Local Solicitor. Husband Blames House Fire."

Rachel died of a heart attack. Her husband, Leonard, believed the fire that had burned down their house a year previously contributed in part to her death. Although the family had recovered financially, Leonard said that his solicitor wife had been in a constant state of stress since the fire. She had lost many personal items of sentimental significance, including photographs of her mother and letters from her grandmother, who had both been survivors of a Nazi concentration camp. Rachel had been unwell and unable to work for a while and had been receiving medication for high blood pressure and depression.

I can't tell you how quickly my good mood disappeared. Was I to blame? Surely Rachel would have discovered the existence of the parcel that her mother left to mine? And surely it was not my fault that the fire had destroyed her birth certificate and, in requesting a new one, she found out the truth of her birth? But still I felt a burden of guilt. Gerry relieved me of some of this.

"Surely it's Hazel's fault in a way, not yours. She should have told Rachel the truth."

"Not the whole truth. I told her she'd been adopted. But she wanted to know about the adoption papers."

"Hazel could have told her something. She was good at making up lies."

"What lies?"

"Come on, Siân. Don't you think it's all a bit far-fetched, her story?"

"No." I shook my head. "I remember Lance. I remember Grant. I remember the scandal of the sudden second wedding. I remember Grant's death and the trial. That's all true, Gerry."

"All right. All right."

"We still have a problem," I said.

"How?"

"What if her husband or her children see her birth certificate? And query it?"

"The problem is *not* ours, Pandora," he said firmly.

"Don't you think they have the right to know the truth?" I asked.

"Leave them with good memories of their mum. Don't muddy the waters."

I had destroyed Hazel's story of her life. Was that right of me? Could I re-tell it, incorporate it into a story of mine?

I wondered if Avril was still alive. She would be in her late seventies. She and her husband Andy (or Andrew) had moved to Coventry—they might still be there now. It would be difficult to find them, but not impossible. Phyllis and Sarah lived in the Midlands. Perhaps they'd help me in my search.

AUTHOR PROFILE

Mary Thurlow was born in Merthyr Tydfil and raised in the mining village of Llanbradach in the Rhymney Valley. She is married to Michael and has two grown-up children and four grandchildren.

An avid reader, she has always wanted to write stories but started late in life after bringing up her family, pursuing a teaching career and becoming actively involved in the local community. After a lengthy spell in Essex, she and her husband have returned to South Wales, and she is intent on achieving her life-long ambition. This is her first full-length book.

Publisher Information

Rowanvale Books

Rowanvale Books provides publishing services to independent authors, writers and poets all over the globe. We deliver a personal, honest and efficient service that allows authors to see their work published, while remaining in control of the process and retaining their creativity. By making publishing services available to authors in a cost-effective and ethical way, we at Rowanvale Books hope to ensure that the local, national and international community benefits from a steady stream of good quality literature.

For more information about us, our authors or our publications, please get in touch.

www.rowanvalebooks.com
info@rowanvalebooks.com

Lightning Source UK Ltd.
Milton Keynes UK
UKHW010007301019
352543UK00001B/51/P

9 781912 655458